"Why do they call you the great peacemaker?"

Ross's question was the last straw.

"Because that's what I am!" Marnie shouted in frustration; then she stilled suddenly, shattered by her loss of control. Dammit. What was the matter with her? "Because that's what I am," she repeated in a soft, puzzled whisper.

Ross's brows twitched at the bewilderment in her eyes and without planning he reached out and stroked her cheek lightly. Marnie jumped at his touch, then slapped his hand away.

"I am not one of your models!" she said curtly. "And I hate to be manhandled!"

The force of his eyes immobilized her. "I doubt that you've ever been handled by a man, Miss Weston," he said flatly. "But when it happens, I guarantee that you won't hate it. You're not the type!"

MELINDA CROSS would love her readers to believe she was kidnapped as a child by an obscure nomadic tribe and rescued by a dashing adventurer. Actually, though, she is a wonderfully imaginative American writer who is married to a true romantic. Every spring, without fail, when the apple orchard blooms, her husband gathers a blanket, glasses and wine and leads Melinda out to enjoy the fragrant night air. Romantic fantasy? Nonsense, she says. This is the stuff of real life.

Books by Melinda Cross

Don't miss any of our special offers. Write to us at the following address for information on our newest releases.

Harlequin Reader Service
901 Fuhrmann Blvd., P.O. Box 1397, Buffalo, NY 14240
Canadian address: P.O. Box 603,
Fort Erie, Ont. L2A 5X3

MELINDA CROSS

king of the mountain

Harlequin Books

TORONTO • NEW YORK • LONDON
AMSTERDAM • PARIS • SYDNEY • HAMBURG
STOCKHOLM • ATHENS • TOKYO • MILAN

Harlequin Presents first edition March 1990
ISBN 0-373-11247-5

Original hardcover edition published in 1989
by Mills & Boon Limited

CHAPTER ONE

MARNIE stood at the broad plate-glass window, staring up at the looming white pyramid of Mount Hazard. Even from the warm confines of the base gondola station the mountain looked cold and forbidding, and every bit worthy of its name.

'I think you're probably a little overdressed, miss.' The station's elderly master technician joined her at the window, nodding with a slight smile at the bulk of her snowmobile suit. 'Even at the top, it won't drop much below freezing until after dark; not with this low pressure system moving in.'

Marnie glanced up at the old man's ruddy, weathered features and favoured him with one of her rare smiles, partly because he was the only human being who had paid her the slightest attention since they had arrived over an hour ago. 'December in the Rocky Mountains sounded pretty intimidating back in a Manhattan highrise. I decided to come prepared.' The quilted black shoulders of her heavy suit lifted in a sheepish shrug.

'Nothin' foolish about being prepared. Especially not here; not at this time of year.' He squinted up at the mountain. 'The old girl can dazzle you one minute and kill you the next, if she's a mind to.'

'The "old girl"?'

'The mountain, of course. Ships, storms, mountains
. . . they're all female. Tough as nails and fickle as the
wind, just like any woman. And the man who turns
his back on anything female is just a plain fool.'

Marnie smiled at the gentle ribbing, refusing to take
offence. 'Don't tell me you're a woman-hater.'

His old eyes sparkled with amusement. 'Hell, no,
I'm not. Been married going on forty years now, to
one of the best women ever walked God's green
earth.' He hesitated, then winked broadly. 'But you
can bet your life I never turned my back on her.' He
took a seat on the broad cement sill that ran the length
of the window and leaned back against the glass. 'So
tell me, young lady,' he folded his arms across his
chest and arched one brow up at her, 'what are all you
city folks doing way out here in the middle of nowhere
this time of year? You and your friends sure didn't
travel all the way from New York City for a gondola
ride up a mountainside.' He jerked his head toward
the nervous trio perched like fidgeting birds on one of
the wooden benches that lined the walls of the small
building. 'And if you don't mind me saying so, those
three sure are an odd-looking bunch.'

Marnie glanced over at the threesome and
suppressed a chuckle. In Manhattan they were the
epitome of chic sophistication, envied wherever they
went as the fashion world's privileged élite; but in
Colorado they were simply odd.

'They get paid to look like that,' she whispered
conspiratorially. 'In New York City, the odder you
look, the more money you get. And silly as it sounds,
we *did* travel all this way to ride up your mountain.

See that man over there?' The old man's eyes followed her gaze to the pale, jittery figure on the bench, so slightly built that he could easily be mistaken for a young boy. 'That's Tommy Hammond. He designed all the clothes those two women are going to pose in on top of Mount Hazard.'

'He's a clothes designer?' The old man looked sceptical.

'One of the best,' Marnie admitted grudgingly. 'You could probably buy a house in the suburbs for the price of one of his evening gowns.'

The old man snorted and shook his head. 'Now don't you try to tell me those sickly-looking creatures sitting with him are going to trot around on top of Mount Hazard in *evening gowns*. Not in the middle of December. Not with a blizzard coming. You take a good look at this face, missy, and you'll see that no fool lives behind it.'

Marnie laughed, partly at his disbelief, but mostly because he'd called the two highest-paid models in the country 'sickly-looking creatures'. 'Tommy was the one who insisted on the location,' she told him with a smile. 'He wanted the contrast—off-the-shoulder gowns in front of panoramic winter view from a mountain top.' She sighed briefly. 'We waited three weeks for this blizzard they've promised. Tommy Hammond never settles for the artificial if he can get the real thing, and Tommy wanted snow.'

'That's just plain crazy,' the old man muttered. 'Flying all the way out here to take pictures of half-naked women in a snowstorm on top of a mountain.' He shook his head, exasperated. 'Well, what on earth are you doing with those fools, girl? Surely you're not part of all this nonsense?'

'Oh, I'm afraid I am.' She smiled, wondering if he would understand all the fancy titles that earned her such a handsome salary, deciding finally to make it simple. 'I'm the make-up person.'

He rose stiffly to his feet, glanced over at the unadorned faces of the models, shiny now with protective cream, then back at her. 'You mean to tell me you made them look like that on purpose?'

This time Marnie couldn't contain her laugh. 'No, no,' she whispered through a grin. 'They were born looking like that. I haven't started on them yet.'

White, winged brows lifted, then dropped in a mystified frown. 'New York City must be even stranger than I thought,' he mumbled, shaking his head as he walked away.

Marnie turned back to the window, a little disturbed that even a stranger had sensed she wasn't really a part of the group she travelled with. It was her fault, of course. Tommy and the models would have welcomed her into their little social circle, shallow though it was. She was the one who always chose to stand alone, much as she did now, distancing herself as much physically as she did emotionally. You had to do that. It was important to remain just a little apart, just a little reserved, because otherwise people attached themselves to you, and then before you knew it you were involved, and emotional involvement was a terrifying thing.

A flutter of movement outside caught her eye, but she had to squint to bring the distant gondola into focus, and for what seemed like a very long time it was only a speck of red against the mountain's snowy face. Dear lord, it looked so tiny, so fragile, like a ladybird dangling helplessly from an invisible string. Slowly, slowly, it descended cables impossible to see from such a distance, and Marnie felt her stomach tremble at the thought of the ride to come.

'It's on its way down,' she called over her shoulder, eyes still locked on the gondola's tedious descent. The glass reflected the sinuous rising of one of the trio behind her, distracting her momentarily from the scene outside.

Even though Marnie was taller than most women, being approached by the six-foot-three Tiffany Child was a little like being stalked by a skyscraper. She frowned when their two reflections stood side by side in the glass. Next to Tiffany's shimmering halo of blonde and towering glamour, her own cap of glossy brown hair seemed suddenly dull, her presence ordinary. She felt like a plain brick house standing in the shadow of a glass and steel highrise.

Tiffany squinted up briefly at the spot of red that was the gondola, then relaxed her features in automatic vigilance against any expression that would engrave future lines in her impeccable skin.

Marnie tried not to look at her. She always tried not to look at her, but it was a futile effort. One *had* to look at Tiffany Child, and the compulsion never lessened with time.

She was the most colourless human being Marnie had ever encountered, and, although that should have made her unattractive, it somehow had the opposite effect. The pale hair, the translucent skin, the cold, ice-blue eyes—all combined to create an ethereal image; a woman who was more spirit than substance, and therefore exquisitely fragile. And that was the biggest hoax ever perpetrated on the American public, Marnie thought with a wry smile. Tiffany Child, for all her delicate beauty, had a vicious mean streak and a cruel tongue, characteristics she concealed skilfully in the presence of people who had something she wanted. She was kinder to Marnie than most, partly because the quiet attractiveness of the brunette presented no threat of competition whatsoever, but mostly because Marnie's placid nature precluded cruelty. There was no satisfaction in striking out at someone who absolutely refused to strike back, whose calm exterior could not be ruffled by even the most determined efforts. Although Tiffany didn't necessarily admire such passivity of character, she was somehow forced to respond to it.

She blew an impatient puff of air through her perfectly chiselled lips, then shielded her eyes with one hand as she looked up at the distant gondola. 'Well, dammit, it's about time that bastard got this show on the road,' she muttered.

Marnie winced involuntarily. Even after all the hours she had spent with Tiffany, it still startled her to hear such language spew from the mouth of a woman who looked more angel than mortal.

'Better clean up your act before you meet the king, Tiffany. From what I hear, he's every bit as difficult to work with as you are. You may have met your match.'

'Like hell,' Tiffany grumbled, actually insulted to think someone might exceed her own reputation for temperament. 'He's just another egomaniac photographer, convinced that the drivel he produces by pushing a button on a black box is art. Despicable lot, every one of them.'

Marnie chuckled. 'According to the critics, his photographs *are* art. And as for being despicable, his models may hate to work with him, but they certainly seem to love sleeping with him.'

'Oh, Marnie, really. You've been reading those trashy magazines again. When are you going to stop believing that garbage? Ross Arnett is just another photographer, and worse than that, just another man.'

Marnie grew serious. 'You're probably right about the last part, but he's not just another photographer, Tiffany. He can do for your career what he did for Cari Blake's, if you play your cards right.'

'He took a perfectly *awful* photo of Cari! No make-up, no lighting . . . she looked *terrible!*'

'She looked *real,* and that's what got her the screen test for her first movie. Look at where she is now. Number one box-office draw, and all because Ross Arnett's photograph made the producers sit up and take notice.'

Tiffany stared down from her great height at Marnie's earnest expression. 'You think I should hit on him, don't you?'

Marnie clapped a hand to her forehead, exasperated by Tiffany's single-minded reasoning. 'In the first place, Tiffany, that would be like telling a fish to swim, and in the second place, that isn't the way you get everything in this life, you know.'

'Really?' Tiffany arched one brow. 'It's worked very well up to this point.'

Marnie sighed helplessly and turned back to the window. There was no way to penetrate Tiffany's catty stubbornness, and besides, how could you argue with the kind of success she'd already achieved? Her looks had taken her to the top of one profession already, so why on earth should she try at this late date to cultivate anything as unnecessary as a personality?

She shrugged away Tiffany's first tap on her shoulder, then turned reluctantly when it became more insistent. 'I'll get what I want from Ross Arnett, Marnie,' she said softly. 'You just pay attention, and I'll show you how it's done.'

'I don't have to pay attention,' Marnie replied flatly. 'I've seen you at work more times than I care to remember.'

'You ready for your little ride, missy?' The elderly station master walked up behind the two women, and smiled at Marnie when she turned around.

'Is it time already?' she asked nervously, battling a fear of heights that had been with her for as long as she could remember.

The old man nodded kindly, seeing her fear as clearly as if she had stated it aloud. 'Gondola should be down in ten minutes or so, but I thought you might want some time to freshen up before you load. It's a good thirty-minute ride to the top, you know.'

'Thirty minute?' Marnie whispered. 'That long?'

'She's a full-grown mountain, missy. Five miles

to the top by the hiking trail, but that's because it has to twist around so much. Thirty minutes straight up in the gondola. Not so far, really. You'll enjoy it.'

'Want to bet?' Marnie whispered sceptically, and he laughed.

Tiffany went back to the bench to gather her things, but Marnie seemed frozen to the spot.

'If it makes you feel any better,' he said confidentially, 'I don't think that big photographer fellow liked the ride much, either.' He peered past her head out the window. 'He rode up with his equipment earlier, and looks like he decided to wait up there instead of making another trip.'

Marnie glanced over her shoulder at the gondola, clearly empty now, and shuddered. Somehow, knowing that a man wouldn't risk the trip twice didn't make her feel better at all.

'I'll tell you what, missy. You can be my radio operator, how about that? You'll be so busy chattering you won't have time to look down once.'

'Radio operator?'

'That's right. There's a radio in the gondola, a d another up top in the restaurant. Usually we send one of our own people up with a group, but Bill and I are the only ones here this week, being the end of the season and all. Takes both of us to run things down here. Just let me know how things are going on the way up, then keep in touch from the top in case this weather front moves in faster than expected. Can you do that?'

Marnie nodded mutely, brown eyes widening even further with every minute that ticked by. She jumped when he reached out with a beefy arm to give her a quick, reassuring hug.

'Well, come on, then. I'll show you how to run the thing. Smart girl like you shouldn't have any trouble with it. All you do is push a button and say, "Come in, Buzz," and there I'll be, hanging on your every word.'

'Buzz?'

'That's my name, girl. And what's yours?'

She took a deep breath and tried for a smile. 'Marnie,' she sighed. 'But you can call me Chicken.'

CHAPTER TWO

THE GONDOLA ride was nothing less than a nightmare. The awful little box swung with every gust of wind, and bounced at each junction of the overhead cables with the monstrous, robot-like support stanchions. Marnie sat huddled over the radio controls in the front of the cab, facing forward, her eyes squeezed as tightly closed as possible. Occasionally Buzz's voice would crackle through the speaker, asking what marker they were approaching. Marnie's eyes would fly open for as long as it took to read the big black numbers stencilled on the stanchion just ahead, then slam shut again.

She was convinced that the gondola had been overloaded. Four people, trunk after trunk of clothes and make-up—any fool could see that it was too much weight for those tiny little cables to support. All it would take was just one bump too many, just one more gust of wind, and the wires would snap and they would all plummet to their deaths. She had the scenario all worked out in her mind, right down to the public mourning of Tiffany Child, and the very private grief of the parents of a little-known make-up artist by the name of Marnie Weston. And her death would be meaningless. 'Four Die for Fashion.' The ludicrous headline popped into her head and simply refused to go away. This was all Tommy's fault, that jerk. They could have shot the layout in the safety of some Manhattan studio, with painted backdrops and artificial snow, but oh, no! Tommy Hammond had to have realism, and now he was going to pay for it with his life, not to mention hers. She was so furious with him that she hoped he wouldn't die on impact; she hoped he'd live long enough for her to crawl over and kill him personally.

After what seemed like hours in the air, Buzz's voice called out merrily, 'Well, you're almost there, missy. Two more markers and you'll be on solid ground again.'

Marnie almost fainted, she was so relieved, and for the first time since the gondola had lurched away from the base station she found the courage to open one eye and peer downward through the side-window. Her stomach rolled immediately at the sheerness of the drop. Even now, this close to the peak, the mountain fell away so sharply that solid ground seemed miles beneath them.

'Why, you little bitch!'

Marnie spun in her seat at Tiffany's shrill exclamation, and was immediately sorry. Even that little movement made the cab sway sickeningly. She closed her eyes briefly, then focused on the figures behind her. 'Now what are you two fighting about?'

Tiffany was leaning forward in her seat, wrinkles forgotten as she scowled across the narrow aisle at Bett Sommers, clearly the number two model for this particular layout, but nevertheless Tiffany's worst competition for the future.

'*We're* not fighting about anything.' Bett drawled, batting slanted, green eyes in Tiffany's direction. 'The almighty Miss Child is just a bit oversensitive about her age, that's all.'

Tiffany shot to her feet and lunged toward Bett, and the gondola swayed dangerously. Marnie felt her heart leap to her throat as she grasped the metal armrests of her chair.

'Sit down!' Tommy yelled, grasping Tiffany's arm and jerking her back into her seat. 'You two can tear each other's eyes out later, if you like. *After* the shoot.'

Marnie blessed Tommy silently as she waited for her heart to slow down, then cursed him again for dreaming up this project in the first place. Shooting on top of a mountain in the middle of winter was bad enough; but shooting Tiffany Child and Bett Sommers in the same layout was a certain formula for disaster. They were frighteningly similar in appearance and temperament—Bett's hair had a little more gold in it, and her eyes were a startling green instead of Tiffany's frigid blue—but their bone-structure, carriage, and that mutual expression of bored haughtiness, made them almost mirror images of each other. With one glaring exception. Tiffany was approaching her twenty-seventh birthday—dangerously close to old age in the brutal world of high fashion—and Bett, a glossy twenty-one, never missed a chance to mention it.

Marnie wondered which one would push the other off the top of the mountain first, and decided that, at that particular moment, she didn't really care.

'I'll kill the next one of you who jiggles this damn

thing,' she muttered, and the threesome laughed together to hear such a preposterous threat from the one person they could all count on to smooth over trouble, not create it.

'Sure you will, Marnie,' Tommy chuckled, nodding to see Bett's and Tiffany's faces relaxed once again, marvelling at Marnie's gift for defusing any situation that threatened to explode.

Marnie gritted her teeth at the gentle mockery, a little frustrated by her inability to intimidate anyone, then shrugged in resignation. To her, anger was a fleeting, unproductive exercise at best—like most emotions—and she'd learned to tolerate it in others and control it in herself long ago. By now she was a master at excusing the bad behaviour of others. Tiffany couldn't help being temperamental because she was insecure. Bett couldn't help being unpleasant because she was still second-best. Tommy couldn't help being eccentric because he was an artist. And Marnie couldn't help being forgiving because John and Ethel Weston had brought her up that way.

She sighed miserably, because kindness sometimes seemed the worst curse of all, but then the gondola lurched one last time and settled, and suddenly life was much too sweet to bear a single complaint, simply because she had survived the trip up the mountain.

'We made it, Buzz!' she called happily into the microphone.

'Why, child, you sound surprised,' came the droll answer, making her laugh. 'Now, there's another radio inside that architectural wonder just in front of you, Marnie.' She glanced up at the concrete block building squatting a hundred feet from the gondola's berth on a flat ledge that jutted from the peak. 'You use that one to check in with me, every hour on the hour, hear? Looks like the snowstorm you asked for is coming in a little ahead of schedule. We don't want you staying up there so long that you risk a trip down in a blizzard. You hear me, girl?'

'I hear you, Buzz. Talk to you later.'

She bent to pull one of the make-up cases from beneath her seat, but stopped in mid-motion at Tiffany's quiet exclamation.

'My God, would you look at that!'

It was the tone more than the words themselves that made Marnie's head jerk up to look out the gondola's side-window, and when she did she understood completely the uncharacteristic awe she had heard in Tiffany's voice. Her mouth formed a circle, as if she would speak, but no words came out.

He stood on the very brink of the shale ledge that formed the mountain top, a full twenty feet above and just to the left of the niche that housed the gondola. His hands were shoved deep into the pockets of light-coloured, loose trousers that buffeted against his straddled legs in the strong wind, printing their shape against the sky. His head was bare, and hair as black as a crow's wing blew flat against his skull. He stared out over the void that fell at his feet, apparently oblivious to the cold bite of the wind. His one and only concession to the weather was a trim black ski jacket, and even that seemed like an afterthought. One had the impression that he didn't feel the cold or the wind; that he was unaware of the perils of his tenuous perch; that he was somehow unaffected by the mundane conditions that ruled the lives of ordinary men.

Marnie had to crane her neck upward to take in the awesome sight of a man who seemed poised to take flight, and for one flashing, fanciful moment she almost believed he would be capable of such of thing. He was born to fly, that man, with nothing but the endless reaches of grey sky behind him, and nothing but the emptiness of thin air before him. He balanced on the rim of the ledge as casually as another man might stand on a small country knoll, inspecting the view.

It's only a man, she told herself, trying to close her mouth, trying to breathe normally, trying to look away, but failing in all those things. Just a man, the thought repeated itself inside her head. Just an ordinary, everyday man. It's the way he's standing there that makes him seem special, just poised on the brink of all that nothingness as if he could lift wings and take flight if he wanted; or maybe it's just the light. Yes, that's what it is, the way the light breaks around his body like that, making him look . . . majestic. But he probably isn't majestic at all, and certainly not as much as he looks. No man could possibly be half of what that man looks like at this moment.

'My God,' Tiffany repeated quietly. 'If it isn't the King of the Mountain.'

Marnie's lips didn't move from their circle, but her mind smiled, because that was exactly what the man looked like.

While they all stood gaping out the gondola window, he turned his head ever so slowly in their direction and glanced down, like a god deigning to acknowledge his subjects. Marnie shivered inside her heavy suit, almost imagining she could feel the touch of his eyes.

The gondola rocked gently as Tommy jumped out, raised one arm in greeting and called out, 'Ross!'

'OK, ladies,' Marnie said without taking her eyes off the man on the ledge, 'last stop.'

She heard the bustle of the girls disembarking, heard Tommy repeat his greeting, but all she saw was Ross Arnett as he made his way coolly down the slide of rocks, never even bothering to look at where he placed his feet. He stared straight ahead, eyes riveted on the gondola as he approached, and, like an adolescent girl with her first crush, she pretended he was looking at her. By the time he was close enough to distinguish his features, she saw that he wasn't looking at her at all. He was looking past the gondola, at Tiffany and Bett. Of course he was. After all, he was only human.

Marnie dropped her eyes and sighed. For a moment, she had hoped that he was more than that.

'Hustle up, Marnie!' Tommy called from outside, and she moved slowly back to the narrow doorway, grimacing slightly when the thick snowmobile suit caught on the edges of the frame. Tiffany and Bett had slipped gracefully through the opening in their elegant furs, but she felt like a big black bubble popping out of a hole one size too small. Her embarrassment increased when she heard a deep chuckle from her left.

'And who's this? Your mascot?'

From anyone else, she would have accepted the gentle tease with good grace, but from the man who stood on the mountain, it stung.

Surprised by her own reaction, she jerked her eyes up furiously, recorded a freeze-frame flash of a pale, angular face that needed a shave, then dropped her head to look at the top of her boots.

'This is Marnie Weston,' Tommy said perfunctorily. 'The make-up artist I told you about. And she's a little testy this morning. Threatened to kill all of us on the way up here.'

'Knowing you, Tommy, you probably deserved it. Besides, riding in that damn thing would make a saint homicidal.'

Marnie glanced up quickly at words that seemed understanding, but Ross Arnett had already turned and was leading the way up the rock steps to the restaurant that seemed to be little more than a house of glass. From the outside, the building's wall-to-wall windows reflected the sky around it; from the inside, the view was breathtaking.

Jaded by many similar sights encountered in their world travels, Tiffany, Bett and Tommy barely glanced at the panoramic scenery, but Marnie couldn't stop looking at it. She stood immobile at a wall of windows with a heavily mittened hand resting lightly on the glass, her black knit cap still hugging her ears and pressing her fringe flat against her forehead. A line of worry divided her brows.

She covered miles with a single glance to the east,

marvelling at the crisp definition of colour up here, somehow more intense than it had seemed below. The white of the snow-capped peaks was starkly brilliant, almost blinding against the darkness of the tree-lines at lower altitudes. Muddy streams of grey cirrus clouds formed wispy crowns for the surrounding mountains, looking like so much dirty lace trailing from a charcoal sky.

'Beautiful, isn't it?'

She'd sensed Arnett approaching, but didn't turn to look at him. 'For the moment,' she replied quietly.

He followed her gaze to the deeper, ominous grey of the western sky. 'You're from the Midwest, aren't you? Minnesota? The Dakotas?'

Now she looked at him, a little surprised by his perception. 'Wisconsin, originally. You have quite an ear for accents, Mr Arnett.'

'It isn't the accent,' he chuckled. 'It's just that all of you look at the sky the same way. No one has quite as much respect for weather as a Midwesterner.'

'With very good reason,' she said, staring at him openly.

His eyes were oddly blue, with that amazing black hair; framed with such an abundance of dark lashes that they would have seemed inappropriate on a less masculine face. But there was no question of masculinity here. If the angular strength of his jaw had not proclaimed it, the straight, hard lines of mouth and brow would have. There was something vaguely threatening about his face, accentuated by the black, unshaven shadow that darkened the lower half of an otherwise fair complexion. Marnie had never seen the contrast of light and dark drawn so sharply, and wondered if it was a physical reflection of the man's soul.

'So,' he mocked her obvious appraisal with an arched brow. 'Do you like what you see?'

'I'm not sure. Frankly, your face is a little hard to read, and more than a little disturbing.'

He frowned at that, then blinked once, slowly. 'So is yours.'

'Well! Mr Arnett!' Tiffany didn't merely approach him, she *absorbed* him, wrapping her thin, graceful arms around his neck from the back, smiling seductively when he turned to embrace her.

There was nothing unusual about this unthinking physical encounter. It was just the way things were in their world, Marnie told herself, puzzled by her unexpected resentment of Tiffany's act of possession and Arnett's automatic response. The beautiful people—the golden children of the fashion industry—always touched, hugged, kissed; and it didn't mean a thing. It was all very calculated, and very, very superficial. So why did she find herself smiling through clenched teeth? Photographers and models were even more demonstrative than most; so instantly, easily familiar with each other that outsiders always assumed they were passionately involved. Marnie, of course, knew better. This immediate communication through touch was necessary; essential, really, to develop the immediate bonding that would ultimately show in photographic proofs. The elegant, envied, beautiful women of high fashion were perversely insecure, and craved even artificial expressions of love from the men who would photograph them. They needed constant reassurance of their beauty, which was the only measure of worth they understood.

It was a bizarre relationship, but such a common one in the business that Marnie had grown used to seeing it. Until now. This time something seemed slightly off-centre. Tiffany was playing out the drama with unusual feeling, looking at Ross Arnett with a slightly startled expression that smacked strangely of sincerity. And there were none of the expected flashing white smiles and easy touches from him, either. He simply took Tiffany gently by the shoulders and held her slightly away, staring deeply, seriously, into her eyes.

'No photographer has done you justice yet, Miss Child,' he said quietly. 'Perhaps no one can.'

For the first time in the three years Marnie had worked with Tiffany, she saw that icy beauty begin to dissolve, to melt away, revealing a slice of something even more substantial in those pale blue eyes; something vulnerable, and deeply human.

The glib responses Tiffany automatically made to compliments every day of her life were lost to her; and with something approaching true dignity she nodded once, then turned and walked away.

Marnie watched Ross follow her with his eyes.

'I'm impressed,' she said flatly, bristling for no reason at all when he turned to her with a cocky smile.

'What you are,' he said after a moment's examination of her expression, 'is jealous. Tell me, Marnie Weston, would you like me to tell *you* how beautiful you are? Would you like me to look into your eyes as I looked into hers, and say something terribly profound, and terribly meaningless?'

'No!' she whispered, horrified at the prospect, humiliated by his mockery.

'I'm glad to hear it,' he said curtly, looking off toward Bett. 'Give me a few minutes with the other beauty and we'll be ready to get to work.' He glanced back at her and shook his head at the cumbersome bulk of her snowmobile suit. 'You look ridiculous in that thing. Take it off. Unless, of course, you look even more ridiculous out of it. I don't think I could stand that.' And then, surprisingly, he flashed a brief smile before walking away.

Normally Marnie's large brown eyes were round and soft and gently expressive. Now they almost disappeared in a furious glare directed at Ross Arnett's back. She felt the ache of a jaw too tightly clenched, the cramp of holding her mittened hands into fists; and then, most surprising of all, the quick, alien flash of uncontrollable anger. It had been so long since she'd felt an emotion so intense that she hardly knew how to handle it.

While she fantasised furiously about all the insulting retorts she should scream after him, the phrase 'Blessed are the peacemakers' popped into her mind. It not only gave her pause; it rocked her. Blessed are the peacemakers, indeed. The quote had been used so often to describe her that it had almost become her trademark. Kind, patient, gentle Marnie; calmly oblivious to the shrieking tantrums of models and designers and photographers alike; saintly in her forbearance; valued above all for her pacific nature in a business fraught with pressured personalities. No insult touched her; no hysteria disturbed her peace; she was the proverbial oil on the troubled waters of any frantic soul. And yet, within moments of meeting him, this one man had shattered that deceptively smooth surface and shown the ugly turbulence beneath. The shock of discovering her own capacity for temper was stunning, and she couldn't quite decide if she hated Ross Arnett for showing her that, or simply because he was such an egotistical bastard.

Stilled somewhat by the revelation of her own nature, she watched from across the room as Ross worked his dark magic on Bett, leaving her every bit as pliable as he had Tiffany. Marnie felt self-righteous contempt at his manipulative nature until she focused on his eyes as he looked down at Bett, and then she frowned, suddenly uncertain.

Whether she wanted to believe it or not, it wasn't total, conscious manipulation. He was managing the girls to a degree, certainly, but there was something genuine about the way he looked at them and talked to them, something warm and caring, and the models obviously sensed it. No wonder they fell so quickly under his spell.

Tommy came over and nodded to where Bett, Tiffany and Ross were laughing together like three old friends. 'Looks as if you have some competition in the peacemaker department, Marnie. Between the two of you, this shoot should be just about trouble-free.'

'Unless your peacemakers decide to war on each

other,' she said cryptically.

'What do you mean by . . . ah, Ross. Finished talking to the girls already? I was just telling Marnie that, aside from her, you're the only person I've ever known who could keep peace between those two. Wish I had your gift with women. Do they always fall all over you like that?'

Ross nodded at Marnie, his lips curved in the beginnings of a smile. 'This one hasn't—yet.'

Tommy's laugh was not intended to be cruel. It was just that the idea of Marnie ever falling all over any man was simply preposterous. Somehow she seemed much too controlled for that sort of thing. 'And she isn't likely to, either,' he chuckled.

Ross took in Tommy's amusement, then raised a brow at Marnie. 'I do believe I've been challenged.'

Marnie affected an expression of impatience. 'Don't take it personally.'

'Oh, but I do,' she heard him say as she walked away.

CHAPTER THREE

THERE was one closed corner in the back of the building, housing two impossibly small bathrooms totally unsuitable for dressing. The kitchen area provided no hope of privacy, either; it was neatly contained behind a circular snack bar in the centre of the large room, and the waist-up activity of anyone working there was clearly visible to any and all who cared to look.

The openness of the restaurant's design would have posed insoluble problems to ordinary women forced to change clothes repeatedly in front of ordinary men; but theirs was not an ordinary gathering of mixed company. The men were even less concerned with models' various states of undress than the models were themselves, simply because modesty had no place in their profession.

Privately, Marnie thought that she would find the circumstances intolerable. To appear half-naked before men who were not moved by the sight robbed a woman of the very essence of her sexuality. She became little more than a mobile mannequin under the emotionless scrutiny and mindless handling of designers and photographers, and perhaps that accounted partially for the pervasive insecurity of most models.

Either Ross Arnett understood that, or he was simply a man of insatiable sexual appetites, for he not only refused to ignore Tiffany's and Bett's nudity when they began changing into the gowns for the first shot; he stared openly at their bodies with frank, suggestive appreciation. The effect on the girls, experienced professionals both, was surprisingly comic.

'Damn!' Bett muttered nervously under her breath, pulling a floor-length blue silk over her head with unusual speed. 'We should hang up some blankets, or something. *Anything* for a little privacy.'

Tiffany obviously agreed with her. The normally unflappable star had actually hesitated before pulling her sweater over her head, awkwardly shy for the first time in her career.

'I don't believe you two,' Marnie said, amused, hands on hips and head shaking. 'You both dress and undress in front of men all the time, year in and year out . . .'

'Not men like *that*,' Tiffany interjected, nodding toward Ross.

'Don't be silly. He's just another photographer. Photographers don't even know women *have* bodies.'

'That one does,' Bett sighed, and the dismay in her voice made Marnie look at her, and then Tiffany, more closely. What she saw in the patrician features of both women surprised her. Virginal modesty would have been laughable in either woman, but it wasn't modesty that she saw in their faces; it was worry—worry that Ross Arnett would see their nakedness, and find them wanting.

'Good grief,' she muttered, rolling her eyes in exasperation. 'All right, all right. Tommy! Dredge up some blankets from somewhere and make us a curtain, or these two blushing violets will never change!'

'What . . . ?'

'Just do it!'

Marnie's uncharacteristic impatience immediately transformed one of the world's most eminent designers to bustling gofer, and within moments Tommy had created a makeshift dressing-room by hanging blankets over the light fixtures that circled the snack bar. Marnie peeked out through a crack in the blankets to glower at the man responsible for all this nonsense. Ross had tipped his chair back on two legs and sat grinning at her mischievously, his arms folded across his chest.

Marnie snapped the blankets closed and turned to her work. The man was absolutely insufferable; and so, come to think of it, was trying to work in the cumbersome snowmobile suit. She'd left it on in subconscious spite after his direction to remove it, but Tommy had turned up the thermostat that controlled the restaurant's electric heat, and it was already uncomfortably warm. Reluctantly, Marnie unzipped the single-piece suit, so thick with padding that it almost stood up by itself, and heaved a sigh of relief when she stepped out of it.

'Now, there's our Marnie,' Tiffany teased. 'Out of the wrapping, but still no shape.'

Marnie grumbled at the gentle ribbing, as she always did, so relieved to be cool again that her good nature was resurfacing.

Most of the women in Marnie's position—women who worked with models rather than modelling themselves—gradually abandoned any and all attempts to present a favourable personal appearance, sensing perhaps that any effort was futile in the company of women born to beauty. Marnie had not yet plummeted to that all-time low in self-esteem, and swore to herself she never would, but there were times that all the effort seemed wasted.

No matter how carefully she dressed, and no matter how carefully she applied her own minimal make-up, the overall effect was unchangeable. She simply could not disguise the lean figure that tended to look boyish, or the diminutive features that tended to look elfin. Her short cap of shining brown hair did little to alleviate that impression, but it fell into charming disarray with a simple shake of her head, and she was too busy a woman to sacrifice such a practicality.

Today she had worn deep rose, a colour that flattered her complexion and contrasted favourably with her dark hair and eyes. Snug corduroy slacks hugged her slim legs, and a matching lightweight sweater carried the colour up to her neck.

'Very, very nice,' Ross teased, poking his head through a gap in the blankets, making Marnie jump and the girls giggle. 'Shame to hide a slender body like that under a snowmobile suit. For a while there, I was almost convinced you were a boy.' His eyes dropped pointedly to her miniature breasts. 'I see now how wrong I was.'

Marnie flushed a bright red that clashed with her sweater, then dashed over to close the blankets with a vicious tug. She heard Ross's mocking chuckle from the other side.

'Quick, Marnie,' Tiffany distracted her with a breathless whisper, 'make me absolutely irresistible. I want that man *crawling* before day's end.'

'Then for the first time in your life,' Marnie scolded irritably, 'you aren't going to get your way. If there's one thing I'm sure of, it's that Ross Arnett has never been on his knees.'

'Maybe not, darling, but there's a first time for everything.'

'You'll have to stand in line, Tiffany,' Bett sniped, and Marnie threw up her hands as the adolescent competition began.

Gowned and bejewelled and heavily made-up for the first layout, Tiffany and Bett donned their heavy furs and boots and went outside into the first flakes of the coming storm without a single complaint. No petulant whining, no expressive pouts, no colourful language—Marnie hardly knew them.

Bundled once again in her black suit and cap, she followed them sullenly, lifting her collar when a blast of icy wind seared her neck. Normally there would have been a raft of peons to perform the menial tasks of snatching coats and boots from the camera's eye, but the gondola had limited the size of their crew, leaving Marnie to handle these extra, unpleasant chores. Under any other circumstances she might not have minded, but Arnett seemed to take perverse delight in barking orders at her, and inwardly she began to fume.

Instead of ruining the shoot, the models' competition for Arnett's attention actually enhanced it. Never had the two women worked so hard at their sensuality, and although Marnie found their obvious posturing juvenile and faintly disgusting, Tommy couldn't have been more pleased. They were creating precisely the image for his gowns he had hoped for.

When Ross finally had the girls posed against the western retaining wall, they exchanged their boots for pathetically fragile evening sandals and doffed their furs. Marnie snatched the coats away from the shot, backed off, then caught her breath, impressed at last by the effectiveness of the location.

Tiffany and Bett were posed facing each other like mirror images, their light hair blown wildly by the cold wind, their gowns billowing around them. White shoulders jumped out from the dark grey of the storm clouds approaching behind them, and the glistening caps of the Rocky Mountains shimmered in the background. The image was one of nonchalant elegance—elegance so totally inbred that it remained unruffled by external conditions—and the models played their silent roles expertly. Both exuded haughty sophistication, heedless of snow or cold or wind, and the camera shutter clicked constantly to capture the mood and the moment.

Ross danced behind his tripod like a dark, mad conductor, black hair flying in the wind, blue eyes strangely alight. Against her will, Marnie found herself mesmerised. The intensity of his expression was echoed in the clean lines of a lean body that seldom remained still. Attracted by motion, Marnie's gaze fluttered from the expressive grace of his long, bare fingers to the tightened muscles of his legs, outlined against the thin fabric of his windswept trousers. She had caught her breath without realising it, and only released it when he finally began to speak.

'Beautiful!' he called out, over and over again. 'Spectacular, Tiffany! That's right, Bett! Challenge her with those fantastic eyes! Damn! You two are breathtaking!'

And on and on went the seemingly endless, familiar litany. Normally the words went in one ear and out the other, but for some reason today Marnie found them particularly irritating. Just when she thought she would scream if she heard one more word of empty encouragement, Ross folded his tripod under his arm and they all rushed for the warmth of the restaurant to prepare for the next shot.

They repeated the exhausting procedure of preparation and shooting three more times before Marnie called a halt.

'That's enough for now,' she answered Tommy's call for the next set. 'We're tired and cold and we need a break. It's time for lunch.'

'Not much team spirit for a mascot,' Ross remarked drily. 'We waste too much time and we won't finish at all. That storm is moving in, young lady, or hadn't you noticed?'

'Of course I noticed!' she snapped, and eyebrows around the room shot up at her tone. 'You think the roses in these cheeks are a sign of good health? I'm damn near frozen to death, and so are they! *You* try running around half-naked out there and see how long *you* last!' She gestured furiously with a hand stiffened by the cold, in spite of her heavy mittens.

The room seemed incredibly quiet after her outburst. Tommy, Bett and Tiffany were all staring at her in silent amazement; Arnett's expression was unreadable.

'Besides,' Marnie went on in a more controlled voice, 'I just talked to Buzz on the radio. He's tracking the storm, and he said as long as we get down by four o'clock there shouldn't be any problem.'

Ross just stared down at her coldly, saying nothing, his eyes every bit as icy as the wind outside. A little unnerved, Marnie turned on her heel and retreated quickly to the kitchen area.

'Unfeeling monster!' she muttered under her breath as she opened some of the cans of soup they'd brought along and set them on the stove to warm. 'Damned idiot intends to kill us all for his precious photographs. Here, Tiffany, Bett. Come stand by the stove. It's warmer here.'

Tommy sidled up to Marnie in that unctuous way of his she knew all too well. 'Can you at least get started on the make-up for the next set while the soup is heating, darling? We'll do the white gowns next, and you *know* how critical the make-up is for that shot.'

'Dammit, Tommy, I'm tired! Even workhorses get a lunch break. It's part of the union contract, or something.'

Artificial or not, when Tommy Hammond chose to look wounded, he put on an award-winning performance. With his pallid complexion and narrow face, he looked miserable at his best; wearing a hurt expression, he was downright pathetic, and Marnie relented.

'Oh, Tommy,' she sighed, ruffling his baby-fine blond hair, coaxing a smile from his thin lips. 'I'm sorry I snapped at you. Just give me a minute to catch my breath and I'll get started.'

'That's my darling,' he cooed, chucking her under the chin, making her mad all over again.

The make-up for the white gowns was indeed critical, and also the most complex work Marnie would do that day. Both Tiffany and Bett had to be body-painted in an abstract rainbow of colours to offset the starkness of the white gowns, and their hair had to be streaked as well. Under the best of studio conditions and with assistants, Marnie's best time had been thirty minutes per model. Today it would take much longer.

A full hour after they had all been fortified with hot soup and coffee, she was still putting the finishing touches on Bett's face.

Ross had been pacing the full rectangle of the building for the past hour, his eyes on the approaching storm, his face reflecting an equally dangerous storm within. He had long since shed his black parka, revealing a black sweater beneath. Layer upon layer of black, Marnie thought once, risking a quick glance in his direction. Was there absolutely no light to the man at all? Had the caring sensitivity she had sensed earlier been just another one of the façades people were always hiding behind in this business? She jerked her eyes away in sudden apprehension when he caught her looking at him.

The image she retained in her mind, in spite of her earnest concentration on her work, reminded Marnie of a slightly mad villain, controlling a destructive temper with a supreme effort of will. Suddenly his pacing seemed ominous, and for the first time Marnie thought of him as vaguely threatening, as if the colour of his clothes reflected the equally dark colour of his soul.

'Could you hurry it up a little?' Bett whispered with unusual timidity, and Marnie realised how very silent the room had become. Arnett's black mood was making them all jittery, as if he were an unstable bomb about to explode.

She spoke a little louder than she had to. 'Bett, you know very well that this is the single most important shot of the whole layout, and I'm not sending you out there until you're absolutely perfect.'

'Then you damn well might not send her out at all.'

Marnie jumped at Arnett's sudden presence at her left side. She hadn't even heard him approach.

'And just what do you mean by that?'

'Take a look outside, lady,' he growled. 'That's a full-fledged blizzard birthing out there, and there's only an hour left before your friend's four o'clock deadline. Either we do this shot right now, or we don't do it at all.'

'But, Ross,' Tommy wailed, hustling over frantically, 'we *have* to do this shot! These gowns are the stars of the collection! The layout will be empty without them! Marnie, darling, *please.*' Tommy clutched at her hand desperately. 'Compromise a little, won't you? You're the great peacemaker, remember? Now, use that inimitable charm of yours on this fellow and save the day, won't you?'

Ross barked out a harsh, unpleasant laugh and grabbed Marnie by the upper arm. 'Now that's probably exactly what I need. A little comic relief. Come on, Marnie. I want to see that charm of yours in action.'

Sputtering a protest, Marnie was literally dragged from the kitchen area to the back of the building, and pushed rudely into the tiny space of one of the bathrooms. Ross slammed the door behind them, spun Marnie to face him with a quick snap of his wrist, then laughed out loud at her red-faced indignation. 'If you expect to charm me with that expression, young lady,' he mocked her, 'you'd better think again.'

Marnie had to bite her tongue to hold back all the high melodrama that made her want to call him something trite, like a brute. Besides, name-calling was a little silly under the circumstances. The limited space had them nearly pressed up against one another, and Marnie had to tip her head back on her neck to look him in the eye.

'Mr Arnett,' she hissed viciously, 'you're the last person in the world I'd waste charm on!' She jerked her arm out of his grasp and fought the impulse to slap his face. It wasn't difficult to talk herself out of that gesture; she didn't have enough room to swing her arm anyway. 'I'm doing my job, just as fast as I can manage under deplorable conditions, and I intend to do it right, even if it is at the expense of your precious schedule.'

She grimaced in anticipation of the thundering roar she expected, then looked up cautiously when it never came. The moment their eyes met, she wished he had chosen to yell instead, to at least release the anger that way. The price of keeping it contained showed clearly in the dark fury of his face, and Marnie felt a slight tremor of real fear.

'The hell with my schedule,' he growled between clenched teeth. 'But I'll be damned if I'll spend another day locked up with this group.'

'With me, you mean?' she asked sharply, but he ignored the question.

'All you need to know is that I want this assignment finished *today*, and you're holding us up.'

Marnie felt the heat in her eyes, and hoped it showed. 'Then let me out of here so I can get to work!'

She tried to move him away from the door by pushing against his chest with both hands, but it was like trying to topple the Rock of Gibraltar by blowing on it, and the feeble effort made Ross chuckle.

'Now, why on earth would Tommy call a hot-tempered thing like you the great peacemaker?'

'Because that's what I am!' Marnie shouted in frustration; and then she stilled suddenly, shattered by the sudden complete loss of her control. Dammit, what was the *matter* with her? She *never* lost her temper, no matter how trying the circumstances. 'Because that's what I am,' she repeated in a soft, puzzled whisper.

Ross's dark brows twitched at the bewilderment he saw in her eyes, and without planning the gesture he reached out and touched her cheek lightly with the fingers of one hand. Marnie jumped at his touch, then slapped his hand away viciously, furious that he thought she could be gentled as easily as one of his empty-headed subjects.

He jerked his hand back in surprise, then a dangerous, raging flush coloured the black shadow of his unshaven chin. At that moment, knowing full well that he wanted nothing more than to return her slap, Marnie had to admire his control.

'I am not one of your models!' she said curtly, in the way of an explanation. 'And I hate to be manhandled!'

He immobilised her with the force of his eyes. 'I doubt very much that you've ever been handled by a man, Miss Weston,' he said flatly. 'But when it happens, I guarantee that you won't hate it. You're not the type.'

Nothing about his face at that moment—not the black line of his lowered brows or the narrowed eyes or the clenched jaw—was half as sinister as the threat and the promise in his smile.

CHAPTER FOUR

THE LAST shot was the worst . . . and the best. The weather had deteriorated with frightening suddenness, and the natural anxiety evident in each model's eyes prompted Ross to change the poses to match the feeling.

'Kneel!' he commanded Tiffany and Bett, and they were obviously every bit as intimidated by his tone as they were by the worsening weather. In a pathetically simultaneous gesture, they both glanced down briefly at their fifty-thousand-dollar gowns, then fell to their knees where they stood in the shelter of the western wall. 'No!' he shouted into the wind. 'Not there! Over *there,* out in the open, right in the middle of the worst of the wind!'

Tommy's and Marnie's mouths both dropped open as the girls scrambled away from the wall's protection without a single protest. Once in the open, dead centre in the middle of the now snow-covered deck, they dropped to their knees obediently while the wind played havoc with their meticulously arranged hair. Desperate for any kind of protection from the frigid blasts of snow and air, they clutched at each other, turning frightened faces to the madman whose camera was already clicking furiously.

'That's *it*!' he shouted, dropping to one knee,

firing off several shots, then falling prone for another angle. 'Keep it up!' His voice was almost lost to the wind as he bounced up and continued a frenzied dance of changing positions. 'This is the finale! At last, at last, the elements bring elegance to its knees! It's perfect!'

Tiffany and Bett huddled closer, arms about each other's bare shoulders, their faces drawn in genuine fear of both the man and the storm, which suddenly seemed one and the same. The wind snatched their hair from carefully placed clips and tossed it mercilessly until it mingled together in a wild halo.

'I'm *freezing!*' Bett finally cried, and Ross caught the shot just as her mouth opened in the frustrated wail.

Bett's face and arms were body-painted in abstract streaks of green that complemented her eyes, as Tiffany was painted in blues. The coloured skin was a bizarre backdrop for the pristine white gowns, even more shocking against the blackened sky and the wind-driven snow. Even as she shuddered at the sheer sadism of exposing the two models to such conditions, Marnie was awed by the effect.

Only when the models' eyes began to water, streaking the coloured make-up, did Ross finally relent and allow them all to scurry inside.

Marnie shivered uncontrollably as the restaurant's warmth enveloped her, wondering how much worse it must be for Tiffany and Bett.

'Quick,' she ordered them, shaking her head at their sodden, pathetic appearance, 'get out of those wet gowns and into something warm.'

Tommy was hopping about on one foot, then the

other, briskly rubbing his hands together, stiff in spite of the gloves he had worn. 'Dear God,' he muttered, peering out the window at where Ross was still gathering his equipment. 'He's stark, staring mad, isn't he? Nearly killed all of us for that layout. And look at him out there—no hat, no gloves, and still he doesn't seem to feel the cold.'

'Well, these two do,' Marnie muttered, bustling about to help the girls change, upset by their chattering teeth and unusual silence. 'Get some coffee, Tommy. Tiffany's lips are absolutely blue.'

A few minutes later a frightening gust of wind followed Ross in the door. He had to lean against it to close it behind him. His expression was urgent. 'Have you talked to the ground station yet?' he demanded of Marnie.

'No, I haven't,' she snapped. 'I've been busy enough as it is, trying to get these girls changed and warmed before hypothermia sets in, thanks to you. You're crazy, you know that? Having them pose out there with no protection in conditions like . . .'

He pushed past her toward the radio set without a single word, leaving Marnie sputtering furiously behind him. He talked in curt, low tones into the microphone, then stomped back toward the cases of clothes and make-up.

'Come on, Tommy,' he said brusquely, bending to shoulder one of the larger cases. 'We have to send down all the baggage and equipment first; there isn't room for that and us in one trip, and we have to hurry. Buzz says we've only got an hour or so before the brunt of the storm hits.'

'Thank God this nightmare is over,' Bett murmured in her first words since she'd come inside. Marnie wondered if she should feel relief that the model was feeling better, or dread that her sharp tongue was warming up again.

Ross paused at the door and directed a pointed glance at Marnie. 'We could use another strong body getting all of this loaded,' he said flatly. 'Especially a strong body dressed for the weather.'

Irritated to be identified simply as a body with a snowmobile suit, Marnie opened her mouth to scream something about not getting paid a small fortune to haul make-up cases around, but thought better of it. Instead, she jammed her hat back on her head, snatched two cases that were entirely too heavy for her, and stomped over to the door. Strong body indeed, she muttered silently, but then he opened the door and the shock of the frigid wind drove all other thoughts from her mind.

'This is ridiculous!' she shouted as she passed cases into the gondola. 'We can't possibly ride this thing down in a gale!'

Ross snatched the last case from her hands and handed it to where Tommy was stacking them neatly in the aisle.

'It's only this bad on the peak,' he shouted back. 'Once the gondola drops fifty feet or so, we won't even feel the wind. There. That's the last of it. Get back into the restaurant before you freeze to death, and call Buzz and tell him to haul this thing down.'

She shuffled back up the slope to the building, banging her mittened hands against her arms to warm them. The aroma of fresh coffee hit her the moment she walked in the door.

'Ah, civilisation,' she sighed, stomping the new snow off her boots. 'Which one of you ugly women knew how to use a coffee-maker?'

A well-aimed styrofoam cup bounced harmlessly off her head, and she laughed as the tension left her. Even the prospect of another gondola ride didn't dampen the relief of finally getting off the top of this mountain.

Tiffany handed her a cup of coffee as she called Buzz on the radio, and she smiled her appreciation. 'Push the magic button, or whatever it is you do, Buzz,' she told him happily. 'We've got all the photographic equipment and baggage loaded for the first trip down.'

'Will do,' his voice crackled back. 'And you be ready to load yourselves as soon as we send it back. I don't like the looks of this storm.'

'There won't be a problem, will there?'

'Not if you're down within the next couple of hours. Probably looks a lot worse up there than it does down here. It's just starting to snow now. But you might find yourself stuck in a hotel here for a day or two, depending on whether the system hits us dead on or passes to the south. Some of the airports west of us are already socked in.'

'I don't care about that, Buzz. I'd spend the winter in Colorado if I had to, as long as it wasn't on top of this mountain.'

Marnie replaced the microphone in its cradle and took her first sip of coffee, savouring the warmth if not the taste. Whichever model had made it hadn't known so much about coffee, after all. It was little more than pale brown water.

The three women took their coffee over to one of the tables and huddled over their cups, staring silently out the window. The faces of both models were shiny with the cream they had used to remove the worst of the body paint, but Marnie noted that their dramatic eye make-up was still intact. A little something for the benefit of Ross Arnett, she thought, suppressing a smile.

Bett was already starting to fidget, shifting in her chair, drumming long nails on the formica tabletop; but Tiffany seemed unusually quiet. Both had shed the wet gowns in favour of the slacks and sweaters they had worn on the way up, but the cream colour of Tiffany's outfit made her appear more ethereal than ever. That was the one thing she had over Bett's youth, Marnie mused as she studied the two models. Bett was undeniably every bit as beautiful as Tiffany, but Tiffany had something extra—some intangible quality that would make her face memorable long after time had taken its toll. Both women looked absolutely exhausted.

Ross and Tommy came in, shook the layer of new snow from their coats and tossed them on one of the benches flanking the door.

'Well,' Tommy said, rubbing his hands together, 'she's on her way down, and I don't know about the rest of you, but I can hardly wait for our turn.'

Unused to the physical activity of loading the gondola, he literally crumpled into the vacant chair next to Marnie, peeling a wet cap off his head and dropping it on to the table. 'It's murder out there,' he grumbled, pushing back the thinning strands of his wet hair. 'I can hardly wait to get off this damn mountain and back to the hotel. I'm going to crawl into my bed, order the biggest steak they've got from room service, and get quietly, happily drunk.'

Her eyes lifted at the sound of Ross's boots, squeaking wetly against the tile as he paced back and forth in front of the glass door, his eyes fixed on the swirling white outside. Now completely relaxed to be only an hour or so from the security of her room at the lodge, Marnie found his anxious pacing mildly amusing. 'Nervous, Mr Arnett?' she asked pertly.

He stopped where he stood and turned slowly toward her. 'Damn right,' he said tonelessly. The snow icing the black cap of his tousled hair was starting to melt in the warmth, dripping on to the shoulders of his black jacket. 'What did Buzz say about the weather?'

'That it was still quiet down at the bottom. Just starting to snow.'

He nodded slowly, then turned to look out the window again.

'Come sit down, Mr Arnett.' Tiffany patted a vacant chair next to her with a tired smile. 'You must be exhausted.'

'I'll get you some coffee,' Bett volunteered, jumping up from the table.

Marnie leaned back and shook her head, amused by the competition, particularly since it seemed to embarrass Arnett. He glared at her briefly, then turned on a smile for the two models. Grudgingly, Marnie had to admit she understood the rush for his favour. When he smiled like that, he was almost irresistible. Unfortunately, he knew it.

Tiffany turned on her own kind of charm as he dropped into the chair next to her. She twisted her torso to face him and blinked with calculated seductiveness. 'Well, Mr Arnett, what's your next assignment? Where do you go from here?'

'New York City, unfortunately.'

'Unfortunately?'

'I'd rather stay here, to tell you the truth. I love the mountains in winter.'

Tiffany nodded knowingly. 'Ah. You must ski, then.'

'As a matter of fact I've never tried it. I just like the scenery.'

'You're in a strange profession for a man who doesn't like the city.'

He looked down at his hands and chuckled. 'I'm in a strange profession, period.'

'Marnie?' Bett called from the kitchen area. She was hunched over the radio console tucked under the counter, her brow furrowed. 'How do you work this thing? That Buzz character is calling, but I can't figure out how to answer.'

Marnie dodged through the scattered tables, banging her hip on the corner of one as she made her way across the room. She rubbed vigorously at what would be a black and blue mark later. She snatched the mike from its cradle and interrupted the crackle of Buzz's voice by pushing the transmit button. 'I'm here,

Buzz. What's up?'

'The gondola is up, that's what,' the reply came back. 'And it doesn't look like it's coming down, either.'

Bett groaned and rolled her eyes in disgust. The sound brought the other three rushing to the snack bar that circled the kitchen area. Ross leaned over the formica surface directly opposite Marnie. 'What's the problem?'

She shrugged and pushed the transmit button again. 'What do you mean, Buzz?'

Static crackled from the speaker as a gust of wind buffeted against the western wall of windows. '. . . blew that transformer right off the line. The gondola runs on electric power, and I'm afraid we don't have any of that any more . . .'

'Buzz!' Marnie interrupted, frowning. 'What are you talking about? Ten minutes ago you said the weather at the base was still fine. How could it knock the power out already?'

'You weren't listening, Marnie. The power problem is sixty miles west, right in the middle of the storm. It's their transformer that blew, but that's the one that feeds power to this whole section of the county.'

Marnie sank into the chair in front of the radio and rested her forehead in one hand. 'I was listening, Buzz. We just didn't receive the first part of your transmission. The static on this thing is terrible, and getting worse.'

They all heard a softly muttered expletive over the speaker, then a frustrated sigh. 'Listen, Marnie,'

Buzz spoke hurriedly. 'Sounds like you're about to lose the roof antenna. Happens almost every time we get a big blow. The radios are battery operated, but if you lose that antenna, we're out of touch, so this may be our last chat for a while.'

Marnie glanced up at Tiffany's sharp intake of breath.

'Go ahead, Buzz. We're all listening.'

'Unless we can find a gas-operated generator big enough to operate the gondola, it's going to stay right where it is, about half-way down the mountain, a hundred feet up in the air. We aren't going to be able to bring you folks down until the power comes back on.'

Everyone groaned in unison except Ross. He was looking off into the distance, eyes narrowed, lips pursed in concentration.

'. . . according to the electric company, it could take as long as two days . . .' Buzz was saying, but static kept interrupting the transmission. '. . . just about everything you need down in the basement. Food, sleeping-bags, wood for the fireplace. The trapdoor's right in the south-east corner, see it?'

Tommy scurried across the room and lifted a section of the tiled floor by a heavy metal ring. He turned toward Marnie and nodded, then disappeared into the floor.

'We found it, Buzz.'

'Good. You'll be fine, then. There's enough food down there to keep an army, but you'll have to keep the fire going. The heat's electric, and it's going to get mighty cold up there before this is over.'

'Let me talk to him,' Ross commanded suddenly, his arm jabbing across the counter to snatch the mike. Just as he grabbed it, a particularly fierce gust of wind rattled the heavy plate windows, and there was a startling clatter on the roof. The radio spat static, then went ominously quiet.

Ross stared down at the dead microphone with an expression of disgust. 'Damn,' he said softly.

'What did you want to tell him?' Marnie asked.

Ross sighed, glanced at Tiffany, Bett, then directly at Marnie, where his gaze rested. 'Nothing.' He looked speculative for a moment, then he smiled. 'Nothing important, anyway.'

'Hey, troops!' Tommy's head popped up from the hole in the floor, distracting the rest of them from the disconcerting prospect of their isolation. 'There's everything we need down there, and a little something extra.' He hefted a case of dusty wine-bottles to the floor next to the trapdoor, and Bett sent up a half-hearted cheer.

'Marnie?' Tiffany's voice had a slight edge to it. 'What time is it?'

Marnie checked her watch. 'Five o'clock. Why?'

Tiffany flashed a smile and shrugged. 'Just wondering, that's all.'

CHAPTER FIVE

'COME on down, Marnie. We can use another pair of strong arms.' Ross was standing at the bottom of the basement stairs grinning up at her, hands on hips, head tipped back on his shoulders. Marnie's heart lurched uncontrollably at the white slash of his smile, and she berated herself for that as she stomped down the wooden steps.

'You look awfully happy for a man who could hardly wait to get off this mountain.'

He shrugged good-naturedly. 'Maybe I decided being snowbound with three women might not be so bad, after all.' His grin broadened. 'Three women, a couple of days—that should work out just about right, don't you think?'

She glared at him when she reached the bottom of the stairs. Obviously his reputation as a womaniser was well deserved. 'What amazes me, Mr Arnett,' she said sweetly, 'is that you can stand upright under the weight of that ego of yours.'

Tommy turned sideways to pass them on his way up the stairs, panting under the burden of an armload of firewood. 'Do you think you two could put off sniping at each other for the time being?' he said irritably. 'I could use a little help here.'

'Bett! Tiffany!' he called out at the top. 'Get your

fashionable butts over here and start hauling this to the fireplace!'

The whine of protests drifted down from above, but footsteps could be heard crossing over to the trapdoor. Marnie smiled involuntarily at the sound of dropped logs and grumbled epithets, then sighed and took a look around.

The basement consisted of a single, small concrete room, barely lit with the white glow of a fluorescent camping lamp Tommy had found. The dark room made Marnie wonder for the first time how they would cope with complete darkness upstairs after nightfall. The sheer height of the mountain prolonged daylight, but some time within the next hour the last of it would be gone. She looked at the cases of canned goods lining one wall, then moved toward a jumbled stack of firewood in the far corner.

Ross reached for her arm and pulled her back. 'Tommy and I will carry the wood. Why don't you sort through the rest of these boxes for something for supper?'

Marnie jerked her arm away, resenting his typically male assertion that in any group of mixed company only a man could take charge.

'I know what needs to be done,' she snapped at him, 'and for your information I spent the first eighteen years of my life hauling wood. If you want to assign woman's work, try it on Tommy. He hates physical labour.'

His face darkened and his eyes narrowed. 'Fine,' he said in a tightly controlled voice. 'Haul firewood, if you like. You can take my place. I have no compunction whatsoever about taking on what you call "woman's work". But remember, you're the one who categorised it, not me. I guess that makes you the chauvinist, doesn't it?' And with that he turned on his heel and began rummaging through the boxes stacked on the floor.

Taken aback, Marnie just stood there for a moment with her mouth open.

Ross turned to look over his shoulder at her. 'Well? What are you waiting for? We're going to need a hell of a lot of wood up there before this picnic's over.'

'Picnic?' Marnie stalked over to the woodpile and began snatching logs. 'Picnic? Is that what you think this is? I'm stuck up here with a neurotic designer, two perfectly useless women, an arrogant, insufferable shutter-clicker who thinks he's Van Gogh with a Polaroid, and you call *that* a picnic?'

'Well!' he said quietly. 'You have a pretty low opinion of just about everybody, don't you? Except yourself, of course.'

Her mouth dropped open in astonishment to hear such an accusation, because he couldn't have been more wrong. Marnie Weston didn't have an unkind word to say about anybody. Everyone knew that. Just because she took the responsibility for others on her own shoulders didn't mean she had a low opinion of them. She was a realist, that was all. She'd been taking care of other people all her life. Somebody had to do it. By the time she thought to tell him that, he was half-way up the stairs with an armful of blankets.

She tried to make carrying the wood look effortless, but it was impossible. She'd been away from the farm too long, spoiled by the city's soft life. Besides, carrying armload after armload of wood up a full flight of steep stairs was a whole lot different than bringing it in from the back porch of her parents' farmhouse. She'd expected the grinding ache in her arms and shoulders, but even her legs felt like someone had opened a drain at the bottom and let all the strength run out. Ross stopped her when she was about to head upstairs with her fifth load.

'That's enough,' he said sharply, snatching the logs from her one by one, stacking them in the crook of his arm as if they were kindling. She made a half-hearted effort to cling to the last log, but the muscles in her arms felt like silly putty. 'You've proven whatever stupid point you were trying to make, so sit down before you collapse.' He shook his head in disgust. 'There's absolutely nothing quite as pathetic as a stubborn woman killing herself trying to prove she has the strength of a man.'

He nudged her gently with one elbow and she literally collapsed on to a seat on a large wooden crate. For one delicious instant she let her arms dangle between her knees, savouring the sensation, then she popped up like a demented jack-in-the-box.

'I am *not* trying to prove anything,' she protested hotly. 'There's work to be done, and I'm doing it, that's all.'

'We're all suited to different tasks, Miss Weston. The mark of true intelligence is knowing what they are. You don't see Tiffany and Bett down here staggering under weights far too heavy for them.'

'I am *not* Tiffany or Bett!'

He paused with one foot on the lowest step and stared at her. 'I never said you were,' he said contemptuously. 'Only a fool would make that mistake.'

Marnie snatched up a pile of blankets and scuttled up the stairs ahead of him, then retreated to the solitude of the tiny bathroom for a few precious moments alone. Someone had lit a single candle on the sink in the windowless room, and she stared at her reflection in the wavering light, mourning the unfortunate combination of genes that had made her thin and dark, hating Ross Arnett for making her feel so inferior. It wasn't fair to compare her to Tiffany and Bett—that was the superficial standard of a superficial man in a superficial business, and dammit, she wasn't going to let it upset her.

She grabbed a paper towel and scrubbed furiously at the sheen of perspiration on her skin, then stared sadly down at the make-up on the towel and wished that she hadn't done that. There wasn't a trace of the façade left now, and, with the make-up cases suspended half-way down the mountain in the gondola, there wasn't a hope of recapturing that precious bit of femininity she found every morning in a bottle. It was one thing for Tiffany Child to trot around without make-up; the colourless porcelain of her skin was natural; but without a concealing coating Marnie's cheeks bloomed with an unfashionable rose. The blush of colour was startling with her dark eyes and hair, and made her feel like a coarse servant in the company of sophisticated gentry.

'Marnie?'

The closed door made it sound like Tiffany's

voice was calling from very far away, and she hesitated a moment before opening it, reluctant to join the others.

'Well, there you are.' Tiffany smiled over her shoulder, then patted the empty space on the floor next to her. 'Come on over. We've got heat at last.'

She'd been in the bathroom longer than she thought. The last rays of twilight had long since dissipated, and the restaurant windows were utterly black. The daylight cold of the room was transformed by the soft golden glow of many candles, and the quality of the light made it seem warm, in spite of the ten-degree drop in temperature since the electric heat had failed.

Whatever else he was, Ross Arnett was a champion fire-builder. He already had a healthy blaze roaring in the huge fireplace that bisected the back wall, and everyone was huddled in front of it, relishing the warmth.

Marnie dropped to her knees next to Tiffany and shivered when the heat hit her. She hadn't noticed the cold seeping into the concrete block building until she felt the contrast of the fire's warmth. She looked briefly at Arnett's back as he threw another log on the fire, then glanced at the enormous pile of wood stacked to one side. Somehow the work had been done without her, after all, and in a way that disturbed her.

'Do we have everything we need from downstairs?' she asked no one in particular.

Ross spun in his crouch and looked at her. His eyes seemed bluer with the fire behind him. 'Plenty of blankets,' he nodded toward the piles of Army-issue green wool scattered around them, 'plenty of food, and wood enough for tonight, at least. We'll probably have to bring up more tomorrow.'

Marnie dropped her eyes and nodded silently.

Tiffany inched closer to the fire, snatching one of the blankets and pulling it around her shoulders. 'God, it's cold already,' she complained, shivering. 'What's it going to be like later?'

'It'll be just fine.' Marnie automatically assumed the role of comforter, but her tone was weary, and a little impatient, as if she'd long-since tired of the responsibilities she carried.

'What time is it?' Tiffany asked again.

Marnie glanced at her watch. 'Almost five-thirty, and I know what you're thinking. Supper time.' She left the warmth of the fire reluctantly and walked toward the chair where she had dropped her snowmobile suit earlier. She had one foot inserted when Ross appeared next to her, shaking his head.

'I wouldn't put that on yet, if I were you.'

She scowled at him briefly, then stepped into the other leg. 'I can take care of myself, thank you.'

'And the rest of the world too, with one hand tied behind your back,' he said shortly. 'Or so you think. But if you put that suit on now, you won't have anything to make you feel warmer later, when it really gets cold. Besides, the stove runs on bottled gas. We'll open the oven door and heat the kitchen area that way.'

She glanced pointedly at his bulky knit sweater. 'Easy for you to say. Your sweater is a lot heavier than mine.'

His eyes dropped to where the thin rose cashmere swelled over her breasts, and smiled lazily. 'I noticed that.'

She blew an infuriated sigh out through her cheeks and stalked into the area circled by the snack bar, leaving her suit behind.

The concoction they ate for their first meal was a chef's nightmare, but at least it was hot, and what Bett disdainfully called 'hearty'. Canned stew, canned beans, oyster crackers and canned pears. In spite of the grumbled complaints, everyone ate voraciously except Tiffany. With typical snippiness, she nibbled on a few crackers, barely tasted the stew, and satisfied whatever hunger she had with the pears.

'You should eat more than that, Tiffany,' Ross admonished her gently. 'You need calories to produce body heat.'

She smiled weakly and shrugged. 'I may eat something else later. For now, all I want to do is sleep. What time is it, Marnie?'

Marnie frowned at the model's inexplicable obsession with the time. 'Good grief, Tiffany. You ask me that every hour. It's six-thirty.'

'Six-thirty?' Tommy yawned, and Bett soon followed suit. 'Why don't we all settle down for a little nap? We can get up later and sing songs around the campfire, or whatever it is one does in situations like this.' For once, he and Bett worked together to settle themselves in front of the fire, and within minutes both were indistinguishable mounds under a pile of blankets.

Tiffany started to arrange a bed of blankets in

front of the fireplace, but her efforts were pathetic. Marnie sighed impatiently, and was just about to move to help her when Ross beat her to it. She bristled silently, watching as he folded two blankets in a makeshift mattress, then covered Tiffany with two more once she was settled.

'There,' he said as he tucked the last blanket gently under her lovely chin. 'That should keep you warm enough.'

She looked up gratefully with those large, ice-blue eyes, and suddenly Marnie was infuriated by her helplessness. 'Thank you, Ross. Will you wake me at ten?'

'Whatever for?'

She shrugged, somehow elegant even lying down, and snuggled deeper into her nest. 'I just want to get up then. Humour me, OK?'

He patted her shoulder. 'My pleasure.'

Marnie got up in disgust and started carrying dishes to the kitchen while Ross piled more logs on the fire. Good, she thought bitterly as she looked over the snackbar at Tiffany's blanketed form, maybe she'll roast there, like a pig on a spit.

The sudden sharpness of such an uncharitable thought astounded her, and she took a quick step backward, as if to escape her own mind. Tiffany had *always* been a little helpless. Sometimes Marnie felt more like her babysitter than her make-up artist, but it had never really bothered her before. At least, not like this. What was wrong with her tonight?

'What are you doing?' Ross exclaimed, sprinting over from the fire, reaching across the snack bar to turn off the spigot Marnie had just turned on. He'd slapped her hand away thoughtlessly in the process and she rubbed at the red mark, brown eyes wide and alarmed.

She took a moment to recover from the shock, then shouted at him, 'I'm washing the dishes, that's what I'm doing!'

The three heads by the fire lifted at the unexpected racket, glanced in their direction, then fell uninterestedly to the pillows of their arms.

'You idiot!' Ross hissed, as if he had just remembered people were trying to sleep. 'The pump is electric. The only water we're going to get is what's already in those pipes, and we sure as hell aren't going to waste it doing dishes!'

Marnie wanted to scream at him, to slap his face, *something;* but he was right, and she knew it. She satisfied herself by glaring at him furiously while she gained control of her temper, then said in quiet, sarcastic tones, 'I wasn't thinking. Thank you for bringing my idiocy to my attention in such a gentlemanly manner.' She rubbed more obviously at the hand he had slapped, and almost smiled when he frowned down at it, deflated.

Damn him, anyway. You could bet he wouldn't have slapped Tiffany's hand like that, or Bett's, no matter what the provocation.

'I didn't mean to do that,' he sighed, shoulders sagging. He lifted his eyes, met the furious hostility in hers, then went back to the fire.

Marnie stayed behind, postponing joining the cosy group by the fireplace as long as she possibly could.

She puttered in the kitchen area, stacking the used dishes under the sink, arranging the canned goods in some sort of order on the counter. When she caught herself about to put the fruit cans in alphabetical order, she almost laughed out loud at her own foolishness. Looking for excuses to avoid the others, Ross Arnett in particular, was understandable under the circumstances, but this was ridiculous.

Remembering how to laugh at herself somehow made her feel better and, yawning, as relaxed as she'd been in hours, she made her way over to the fireplace for a well-deserved, much-needed nap.

Tiffany and Bett were two long, graceful green sausages, sleeping peacefully in central positions that afforded them the greatest benefit of the fire's heat. Tommy was rolled into an impossible tangle of blankets to the right of the women, and Arnett was sprawled lazily on their left. Marnie stood behind them, hands on hips, lips pressed into a grim line as she observed the deep, regular breathing of the four sleeping figures. She should have expected as much. There wasn't a spare inch of fire frontage left for her.

She toyed with the idea of waking them all up with a small tantrum, then opted for the role of isolated martyr instead. She didn't belong in this group, anyway, not really; and it seemed appropriate that she be as physically separated from them as she was mentally. It might not be as cosy on the floor within the kitchen area, but with the small oven on she probably wouldn't freeze to death.

As quietly as she could, she stacked several more logs on the fire, then gathered an armload of blankets and went to make her bed.

The only purpose the open oven door seemed to serve was to block the heat from the floor where Marnie lay. Even with several folds of blankets beneath her, the chill of the tile beneath seeped upward into her bones. She had donned the insulated snowmobile suit before crawling under the blankets, but even that didn't seem to help. She tossed and turned on the floor for nearly an hour, praying for the oblivion of sleep she knew her body needed, and then she quit trying. Even without the physical discomfort, the noise would have kept her awake.

The wind had picked up considerably in the last hour, buffeting the heavy plate-glass windows in a constant dull rumble that was relieved only by the even stronger gusts that actually rattled the windows in their sturdy frames. Occasionally a downdraft swept into the chimney, making a hollow, lonely sound as the rising heat forced it out again. There was an air leak around one of the windows, and, when the wind found it, it whistled mournfully, sending shivers up Marnie's spine. And, if that weren't enough, someone by the fireplace had started to snore.

Gritting her teeth, Marnie rose from behind the snack bar like a blanketed Phoenix. Secretly hoping that it was Tiffany making the abominable sounds, she peered across the room, then sighed in disappointment when she saw Tommy's mouth open. Luckily for him, he looked too pathetic to disturb.

Tightly zipped into her suit, Marnie wrapped herself in two blankets, donned her boots, grabbed a candle, and crept over to a table by the south wall.

She settled into a shapeless lump in the chair next to the window, lit the candle, then gasped softly when she peered outside.

The candle's feeble glow barely illuminated the scene just outside the window, but what she saw was enough to make her shiver and pull the blankets more closely around her. It was impossible to determine how much snow had fallen with the wind whipping it into such formidable drifts, but, whatever the amount, the white blanket lay well over knee-depth on the deck. She glanced quickly over at the western windows and saw that the mountainous drifts were already pressed against the glass at her height. Even as a child in Wisconsin, winter's wrath had never seemed so wildly inhospitable, and she had never felt so small in the face of it.

'Hi.'

She gasped and jumped at the sudden pressure of a hand on her shoulder. 'Dammit, you scared me to death!' she hissed. 'What did you do? Float over here?'

Ross grinned down at her, then set two stemmed glasses on the table and filled them from a dusty bottle he'd had nestled in the crook of his arm. 'I don't think you would have heard me if I'd roller-skated over here. The wind is making almost enough noise to cover Tommy's snoring. Almost. But not quite. Here.' He handed her a glass. 'This is a peace offering, by the way. I woke up and found the rest of us hogging the heat while you huddled over here in the cold. Sorry about that.'

'No need to apologise,' she said quickly, unused

to anyone's concern, and a little embarrassed by it. 'Don't worry about me.'

He chuckled softly and slid into the chair opposite hers. 'It's about time somebody worried about you, isn't it?' She frowned at that, but before she had a chance to respond he tapped her glass. 'Drink up, now. It's a fairly decent burgundy.'

She sipped first, then took a deep, gratifying swallow. Supper had been hot and filling, but salty. 'Oh, that's good,' she sighed, closing her eyes. 'Alcohol's illusion of warmth. Almost like the real thing.'

'Not recommended before going out in the cold,' he said, refilling her glass, 'but it doesn't look like we'll be tempted, does it?'

Marnie nodded grimly and returned her attention to the fury outside. 'I've never seen anything like it.' She pressed her forehead against the glass of the window, pulling back quickly when the cold bit into her skin.

'You haven't seen anything yet. Wait until the storm hits.'

She laughed quietly.

'I'm not kidding, Marnie.' She turned her head slowly to look at him, eyes widening, and he nodded. 'This is just the leading edge. The worst is, as they say, yet to come.'

'That's impossible,' she whispered. 'How can it get worse than this?'

He leaned back in his chair and studied her, wineglass cradled at his chest. She noticed that he still hadn't put on his ski jacket, and marvelled that he could sit there in such apparent comfort while she shivered in spite of her suit and blanket. 'Well, for starters, we haven't had much snow yet. It looks like a lot, because of the drifting, but I'd guess we've only had about a foot. Up at this elevation, four times that amount isn't uncommon in your average storm, and I don't think this one is average.'

'Four feet,' Marnie repeated tonelessly.

'And the wind velocity will increase . . . measurably,' he went on. 'By morning, we won't be able to see out the western windows at all, the drifts will be so high.'

'But those windows must be twenty feet high!'

He smiled at her disbelief. 'You haven't seen many Colorado winters, have you?'

'And I'm beginning to wonder if I'll ever get a chance to see another one.'

'I wouldn't worry about that. This is normal for the mountains, and the people here are used to it. You'll see. In a day or two the gondola will be running, the roads will be ploughed, the planes will be flying, just like always.'

'The trick is to live through the next day or two,' she commented wryly, pouring more wine. 'I grew up on a Wisconsin farm, and we had our share of blizzards . . .' She stopped speaking abruptly and stared out the window, her thoughts far away. '. . . but this is worse. Much worse.'

Ross followed her gaze and nodded, then he smiled. 'Bad as it is, I think it's what I like most about the mountains. One of the few spots left in this world where nature can still put man in his place.'

She looked up with surprise. 'I would have thought

you'd resent being put in your place, by nature or anything else.'

He smiled slowly. 'There's nothing quite as lonely as the belief that you're absolutely invincible——' he paused significantly '—is there, Marnie? As for myself, I like being reminded that the world is filled with things more powerful than I am. Whenever I catch myself thinking that some photograph or some layout is just about the most important thing ever, I come to the mountains, and they straighten out my thinking in a hurry.' He looked away from her and sighed again, frowning. 'I seem to need to come more and more often every year.'

'I didn't know you were an outdoors man,' she said softly. 'None of the articles I've read ever mentioned that.'

'My agent doesn't think that kind of publicity fits the high-fashion photographer image, whatever that is. Lord, it's cold here. What do you say we move back to the fire?'

He stood and turned to lead the way, then stopped and spun to face her so suddenly that she almost ran into him. 'Is it possible that you actually get drunk on two glasses of wine, or are you just tired?' he asked, smiling down at her.

'I admit to the tired part,' she smiled crookedly. 'Why? Am I acting funny?'

He frowned down at her earnestly, then reached out with one finger to touch the end of her nose. 'As a matter of fact, you are. You've actually been civil for the last thirty minutes, and I find that disturbingly out of character.'

She made a face at him, but once he'd turned his back again she smiled.

He made another mattress of blankets next to his, then motioned Marnie to the inside, next to Tiffany. 'Crawl in between us,' he whispered. 'You'll be warmer there.'

She smiled her thanks as she shed the bulky snow-mobile suit, then crawled on to the blankets that still bore the indentations of his body. It was a strangely intimate thing, to sit where he had lain, imagining that she could still feel the warmth his body had left there. And it was blessedly, wonderfully warm with her feet stretched toward the fire and all the bodies in a cosy row to her right. She shivered a little with the anticipation of Ross lying on her left, closing her in. Then she would truly be warm, and safe, and somehow, a part of something bigger than she was. She would belong.

For the moment she remained sitting, propped on arms braced stiffly behind her. She sighed with contentment as she watched him tend the fire. Maybe she'd been wrong about Ross Arnett. Maybe there *was* more to the man than the arrogant egotist behind the camera. Certainly there was nothing shallow about someone who revered the superior forces of nature; nothing superficial about one who intentionally sought out the measure of his own frailty in the shadows of the Rocky Mountains. Perhaps he had been right about her. Maybe secretly, subconsciously, she *did* have an automatic low opinion of everyone associated with their business . . . you're involved in the frivolous world of fashion, therefore you're a frivolous person . . . and that was blatant, unfair categorisation. She had no right to judge him without giving him a chance to demonstrate the kind of person he really was, and because she had unwittingly done that she was suddenly ashamed.

His hair fell across his forehead as he bent to replenish the fire, catching the golden glow of the flames and somehow absorbing it. What had she thought? That he personified the dead black of no colour? And yet that was a falsehood in itself, since black was really the combination of all colours. She could see them all now—reds, blues, browns—reflected in the wayward strands that brushed his brows as he scowled at the careful placement of one log. The strong angles of his profile seemed to capture the energy of the flames, storing it to be dispensed later, bit by bit.

As if sensing her eyes upon him, he turned his head to look back at her. For an instant, she saw herself as he might see her—almost childishly vulnerable with her rosy cheeks and dark eyes that filled her face with the trusting wonder of the very young. Firelight flattered, she knew, and in that brief moment when their eyes first met, a secret part of her, a part she had never fully acknowledged, envied the Tiffanys and the Betts of the world for the very first time.

He removed his boots, then slipped under the blankets next to her, turning and propping his head on one elbow, as she did, so they were face to face. His cheeks and chin were dark with unshaven stubble, and when he grinned unexpectedly the white flash of teeth was startling. 'Alone at last,' he whispered mischievously, and Marnie couldn't help herself. She giggled. He pressed two fingers quickly against her lips, but it was too late.

'Marnie?' Tiffany murmured next to her, so quietly that Marnie thought at first she must be talking in her sleep. The impulse to check on her was strong, but for once she fought it. Please, Tiffany, be quiet! she thought. Don't spoil this for me.

But Ross had already stiffened and was peering over her, past her as if she didn't even exist, at Tiffany's slowly turning form. 'What is it, Tiffany?' he whispered, and Marnie clenched her jaw to hear the same gentle tone she would have used echoed in his voice. She rolled flat on her back and squeezed her eyes tightly closed, trying to shut out the sound.

'Is it ten o'clock already?' Tiffany murmured sleepily.

'Way past that,' Ross whispered. 'Almost eleven. You were sleeping so peacefully, I didn't have the heart to wake you.'

Tiffany muttered an expletive, and Marnie opened one eye when she felt the model struggling to extricate herself from the tangle of blankets. The single curse expanded to a whole string of groggy epithets that made Ross raise one brow. Marnie was used to it. She just rolled her eyes, released a heavy sigh, and sat up to help Tiffany out of the tangle of green wool. Once freed, Tiffany proceeded to stomp about the dark restaurant in her stockinged feet, muttering continually, until even Tommy and Bett had been wakened.

'What the hell?' Tommy asked, propping himself

up on his elbows and looking around sleepily.

'Dammit, Tiffany! Be quiet!' Bett bellowed, jerking her blanket over her head.

But Tiffany would not be quieted, and from the sound of it she was rearranging every stick of furniture in the building. Marnie was just about to jump to her feet and scold the inconsiderate model herself when the clatter stopped and the crying began.

'Marnie?' Tiffany sobbed quietly from somewhere near the door.

Marnie's arms tensed on her chest and she opened her eyes wide, listening.

'Marnie?' Tiffany's cry rose to a wail, and Marnie jumped to her feet and hurried across the room to the model who needed her.

CHAPTER SIX

MARNIE had seen Tiffany in all her guises, each one affected to serve a very precise purpose. There was her little-girl pout, guaranteed to turn the most stubborn antagonist into a sheepish, apologising puddle of jelly; her cold, stony expression, usually employed as a last resort, when there wasn't any hope of getting her own way; and then Marnie's personal favourite, the brink-of-tears routine, particularly effective since it threatened to ruin hours of careful work on make-up. Tiffany knew every trick in the book to get what she wanted, all right, but this wasn't one of them. The tears weren't sparkling on the rims of those remarkable eyes, only threatening to spill—they were running freely down her cheeks already; and for once her beautiful face was screwed up into a very unbeautiful mask of genuine despair, wrinkles be damned.

'My God, Tiffany, what is it?' she asked worriedly, instinctively moving to grab the model's cold hands.

As if she sensed the unseemliness of being comforted by someone whose head barely reached her chin, Tiffany sank on to a chair and dropped her face into her hands. On cue, Marnie stooped to put a comforting arm around her shoulders. Her expression of concern tightened when Tiffany sobbed, 'I can't find my bag!'

'Oh, honest to God,' Bett groaned. 'At least she didn't wake us all up for something silly. Losing her bag, well! That's a catastrophe of major proportions.'

'But it *is*!' Tiffany cried, startling them all into wide-eyed silence. Even Marnie had taken a quick step back, shocked by the desperation in her tone.

After a moment, Ross knelt solicitously in front of Tiffany's chair, placing both hands on her knees. 'Tiffany,' he smiled up at her tenderly, 'why don't you go back by the fire? It's much too cold for you to be up without your coat and boots. If it's that important to you, Marnie and I will find your bag.'

Marie's eyes flew wide, then narrowed as she glanced down at her own coatless body and stockinged feet. Now, why the hell was it fine for her to run around like this, but too cold for poor Tiffany? She met Ross's gaze head-on with a furious stare that spoke volumes. He countered it with a quick, hard frown, then led the sobbing Tiffany back to the fire. To his credit, he returned with Marnie's boots and snowmobile suit, but she refused to be mollified. Suddenly she was sick to death of always being the one who managed; the one who coddled people like Tiffany; the one who was always expected to make things right.

' "Marnie and I will find your bag",' she flung his own words back at him in a mocking hiss. 'It was really good of you to offer my services, but what if good old dependable Marnie decides to let Tiffany find her own damn purse? What then? Why should I trot around freezing my tail off so that she can have a piece of gum, or another shot of lip gloss, or whatever the hell she wants?'

She'd started out whispering, but toward the end of her angry outburst her furious hissing was almost loud enough for the others to hear. In a single motion, Ross pulled her next to him with one arm, turned away from sight of the others, and covered her mouth with his other hand.

Marnie sucked in a startled breath and almost bit him in pure, unthinking frustration.

'You've got every reason to be sick of mothering this crew,' he whispered sharply. 'As a matter of fact, I can't imagine what took you so long to wise up, but frankly, your timing stinks.' She squirmed against him, but he only tightened his arm. 'You've obviously been babying Tiffany for some time, but this isn't the moment to back out. She's damn near hysterical already, and clearly incapable of finding her own bag, as stupid as that sounds, so you and I will have to do it. What I'd like to know is how you got trapped into this ridiculous role. Are you always taking care of other people?'

He released the pressure of his palm on her mouth slightly and she mumbled bitterly, 'Those who can, do.'

'Isn't it the truth,' he chuckled, bending his head to speak directly into her ear. 'But it's a dangerous philosophy, Marnie. Pretty soon you start to think you're the *only* one who can do anything, and you end up a slave to other people, always doing for them, forgetting what it's like to live your own life. The weak ones drain you, sap all your strength.' His breath disturbed the tiny hairs at her ear and made the back of her neck prickle. 'Worse than that, people start to depend on you, like Tiffany, and it gets harder and harder to let them down.' Was it her imagination, or had he moved even closer, until his lips brushed against her earlobe when he spoke? 'She's frightened now for some reason, and you're the one she's counting on, aren't you, Marnie?'

Marnie frowned at the reminder, took a quick, shallow breath, and felt his arm tighten slightly around her shoulders. He was playing her. She knew that, but he was doing it so well. The hand over her mouth eased to one side and cradled her cheek in its roughness. 'It was you she called for, remember,' he murmured against her hair, and just when she felt herself start to sag toward him, to actually fall for this incredible malarkey, she jerked away and spun to face him.

'You can stop pushing all the magic buttons now, Arnett,' she whispered fiercely. 'I'll look for the damn bag, just to put an end to this ridiculous charade.'

He surprised her a little by backing away, his wounded expression so close to perfection that she was almost convinced it was real; but then he shrugged with a nonchalant grin and she spun away to put on her boots and suit.

By the time they'd searched the entire building, carrying candles like eighteenth-century prowlers, it had grown cold enough to force even Ross to put on his ski jacket. He looked truly mad stalking through the building, Marnie thought, with the candlelight playing against the angles of his face, as if it danced disembodied through the darkness. It never occurred to her that she presented precisely the same image.

Oddly enough, they had to wake Tiffany to give her the bad news. No gum, no lipgloss, so sorry, Marnie thought as she shook the model gently, thinking the catastrophe couldn't have been too severe if she'd fallen asleep waiting for its resolution.

'Sorry, Tiffany,' she whispered. Tommy and Bett were both asleep again. 'We couldn't find it anywhere. It was the big tapestry bag, right?'

Tiffany didn't even bother to raise her head. She just lay there on her back, big blue eyes blinking solemnly. 'Yes,' she answered dully. 'It was the big tapestry bag.'

The long lump that was Tommy rolled to face them from Bett's other side. Apparently he hadn't been asleep, after all. 'I remember that one,' he said, nodding. 'I carried it out to the gondola myself. It was so damn big I just assumed it was another make-up bag. Sorry, Tiff.'

Tiffany closed her eyes, but her lips twitched, then curved into the strangest smile. For some reason, it made Marnie shudder to look at it.

'What was in the bag, Tiffany?' she asked carefully, not even bothering to whisper.

Bett groaned in disgust, rolled over and opened bleary eyes. 'Oh, give me a break. Are we still looking for that stupid bag?'

Tiffany was still smiling, but she said nothing. Obviously her expression troubled Ross, too, because he reached across Marnie to shake her gently by the shoulder. 'Tiffany?'

She turned her head toward him and smiled the angelic smile that had made her famous. 'My insulin,' she said quietly. 'My insulin is in that bag.'

The ensuing silence was so total that they all jumped when a droplet of sap exploded in the fire's heat, sending a shower of sparks up the chimney.

'Insulin?' Tommy whispered. 'You're diabetic?'

Even Bett had snapped to a sitting position, and four pairs of eyes locked on Tiffany's face. She nodded once, and the terrible smile faded.

'How could you be a diabetic?' Bett wailed, as if Tiffany had somehow failed them all. '*I* didn't know that. Did *you* know?' she poked Tommy in the ribs. '*Nobody* knew. How could you be a diabetic without anyone knowing?'

The questions were mindless, pointless, and only a measure of the foreboding they were all starting to feel.

'How do you think I stay so thin?' Tiffany chuckled behind closed eyes, and Marnie remembered her selective nibbling at supper. Damn. She'd thought she was just being snippy, that the food wasn't good enough for Tiffany Child; now she wondered if that miserable conglomeration of carbohydrates had included anything a diabetic would be allowed to eat.

Marnie pulled herself to a cross-legged position and turned until she was facing Tiffany. In a way, she wished she would sit up. She looked so frail, already ill, lying there on her back like that while the rest of them talked over her body. She felt Ross rise to his knees behind her and look over her shoulder. 'How serious is it, Tiffany?' she asked quietly.

'Given the circumstances,' Tiffany sighed lightly, 'I'd say it was damn serious. I was due for my next shot at ten o'clock.'

Ross winced and shouldered the guilt of not waking her.

'And if we're really stuck up here for the next couple of days, I'm afraid I won't be getting into that gondola under my own power.'

'What?' Bett jumped to her feet and stood stiff-legged in front of the fire. 'What are you talking about, Tiffany Child? Don't say things like that! Diabetics don't die any more. They take pills and shots and live as long as anybody!'

Had the situation been less serious, Marnie would have laughed at Bett's distress. Even witnessing the reaction herself, she could hardly believe it. Bett Sommers had never seemed capable of any kind of feeling for anyone other than herself—least of all for her prime competitor—but it was clear from her expression that the idea of Tiffany's being truly ill terrified her. Surprise, surprise.

'Take it easy, Bett,' Tiffany calmed her, reaching up to pull her back down with one hand.

Another surprise. Empty-headed Tiffany, facing a life-threatening situation, was taking control, soothing someone else's fears.

'I didn't say I was going to die,' she chided Bett. 'Not if we get out of here soon enough. But if it isn't by tomorrow afternoon . . .' she shrugged sheepishly, 'you'll probably have to carry me out. I'll be in a coma by then.'

Tommy jumped to his feet just as Bett sank down,

and in one of those crazy associations you make in times so desperate that the mind defends itself with absurdities, Marnie thought of them as ducks in a carnival shooting gallery—when one was shot down, the other popped up. 'I'll go and get it,' Tommy declared, lip quivering. His eyes were every bit as wild as the thinning blond hair sleep had spiked away from his head. 'That's all we have to do, you know—get to the gondola and bring back the bag.'

'The gondola is hanging about a hundred feet off the ground.' Marnie reminded him gently. 'There's no way we could reach it.'

Tommy sank to his knees, his thin face working furiously in an effort not to cry. Much to the horror of everyone, he failed. 'My God, my God,' he sobbed into his hands. 'It's all my fault. I loaded that bag myself . . .'

'Stop, Tommy, stop. It's nobody's fault.' Tiffany had moved with surprising quickness, up from her bed, over to embrace the guilt-stricken designer.

Bett had started to cry too, and soon Tiffany was hugging them both, soothing them with her words and her touch. Marnie just looked on, astonished by the depth of feeling erupting from people she had always thought incapable of emotion. She jumped when she felt Ross's hand on her shoulder. He'd been so quiet, she'd forgotten he was behind her.

He squeezed gently, as if communicating to her first, then spoke offhandedly. 'It's really not such a disaster. I'll just hike down to the base station, get some insulin from the local pharmacy, and bring it back up.'

Oh, sure, Marnie thought, flabbergasted that he would even suggest such a thing. Hike down a mountain in the blizzard of the century, run on over to the local chemist, then trot back up the mountain again. Who was he kidding? They'd both seen the fury of this storm from the window. She started to jerk around towards him, but his grip on her shoulder tightened and held her immobile.

As it happened, she didn't have to remind anyone of the conditions outside. The wind chose that moment to hit the building with a gale-force blast that rattled the windows with alarming fury.

'You can't go out in that,' Tiffany whispered, her eyes so wide they seemed to absorb her face.

He jerked his head in casual dismissal. 'It sounds a lot worse than it is. The wind is always stronger on the summit. Besides, I stomp through the mountains quite a lot, actually. I'm used to it.'

Tiffany's, Bett's and Tommy's faces were all turned toward him, each sceptical, but each grasping, too, for the only hope offered. Marnie hated them in that moment, every one of them. They were all helpless children, looking to someone else, someone stronger, to save them from the consequences of their own mistakes. Ross's words echoed in her mind—'The weak ones drain you, sap all your strength . . .'—and now she realised that he really *had* meant those words, he hadn't just been playing her, and he'd been talking about himself, too. But this wasn't just a simple bag-finding expedition; it wasn't just his strength he was risking. It was his life.

'You can't . . .' she started to say, then gasped when

his fingers pressed painfully into the flesh of her shulder.

'You can help me get ready, Marnie,' he said brusquely, pulling her to her feet, dragging her away from the others. 'We'll go down to the basement and gather the things I'll need. Tommy, you stay here with the girls and keep the fire going.' And before anyone could say another word he was half-way to the trapdoor, tugging Marnie along with him.

Once they were out of earshot he pushed her firmly down into a chair. 'I'll go back for our coats and boots,' he said softly. 'You stay right here, and save anything you want to say until we get downstairs.'

She was too shocked by the sudden turn of events to say anything anyway, and just sat there obediently while he hurried back to the fireplace and gathered their things. At least he hadn't lumped her in with 'the girls', although she wasn't sure if that was good or bad. The only thing she was sure of was that he absolutely could not try to walk down the mountain in this storm, and that she was the only one who would try to stop him, the only one who really knew how lethal a blizzard like this could be. Six years ago she'd watched another man walk alone into a blizzard, and that man had never come back. She wasn't about to let that happen again.

She closed her eyes to block the memory, but it came anyway, as it always did. In her mind's eye she could still see windscreen wipers batting impotently against wind-driven snow; she could still feel the sickening lurch of the car skidding from an icy roadway into a ditch; and she could still hear her own voice begging her brother not to leave the car to look for help . . .

'Marnie?'

She jumped at the pressure of Ross's hand on her shoulder, then slipped quickly into her boots and suit and followed him down to the basement. She watched the black hair on the back of his head bounce as he descended the stairs, and struggled to make sense of the feelings that were tearing at her, and terrifying her. It was more than just a fear of having what happened to her brother happen to someone else. It was fear for this particular man, above all others. Perhaps it was because she had seen something of herself in him in that first moment as he stood on that cold, windy ledge, totally unafraid, and totally alone. Or perhaps it was because she saw more than that in the genuine caring he felt for others, an emotion she envied, because she couldn't make herself feel it any more. Or maybe it was just because he had the uncanny ability to make her mad, to make her feel *something*, and no one else had been able to do that for a very long time.

'I won't let you go out there,' she told him once they were downstairs.

The single camping lamp didn't shed much light in the black room, but it was enough to highlight the desperate concern on her face.

Ross frowned earnestly at her for a moment, then his features relaxed in a delighted smile. 'You're worried about me,' he teased. 'That's certainly an improvement in our relationship, isn't it?'

'Stop joking about it!' She slapped ineffectively at

the down-filled jacket covering his chest. 'It isn't funny! You could get lost out there! You could freeze to death!' And the more she protested, the more desperate she became, because she'd said those same things to Jimmy and they hadn't stopped him, and now it was happening all over again, but this time she knew the ending, and he still wouldn't listen . . .

'That's a little melodramatic, Marnie, don't you think? It's just a little winter storm . . .' But those were almost the exact words Jimmy had used, and Marnie pressed her hands to her ears, refusing to listen to them again, but she still heard them inside her head, only it was Jimmy's voice . . .

She was slapping at his chest with both hands without realising it, then with her fists, choking back tears of frustration because one storm had already taken her brother, and now another was threatening this man's life and she didn't even know why she cared so much, and then suddenly he grabbed her fists and jerked her against his chest and hushed her sternly, and she realised that she had said all that aloud.

Her lips remained parted on her last word, and when her shoulders finally sagged in a long, shuddering sigh, he released her hands and pulled her deeper into the circle of his arms. She let her head rest against his chest, just for a moment. 'Your brother died in a storm like this?' he whispered into the hair at her forehead.

She gulped and nodded, and her cheek made a whistling noise against the nylon of his jacket. 'Six years ago. He was driving—too fast, like he always

KING OF THE MOUNTAIN

did,' the words came out in a choked whisper. 'We went in the ditch; Jimmy made me stay in the car while he went for help . . .' Ross waited patiently while she took two great breaths. 'The snowplough found me a few hours later, but Jimmy got lost . . . we didn't find him until . . . until . . .'

Over her head, Ross's eyes closed in a pained expression. 'I'm sorry, Marnie. I didn't know.'

She pressed her head deeper into his jacket, and his arms tightened slightly around her.

'That won't happen this time,' he said softly. When he felt her body tense, he lifted one hand to stroke her hair. 'I know these mountains in winter, and I'll be better dressed, better equipped than Jimmy was.' The sharp sound of her short breaths echoed in the quiet room. 'Besides, Marnie,' he pushed her away slightly to look her in the eye, 'I don't have a choice. I have to go.'

Her mouth opened to form an angry denial, but he touched it gently with two fingers to keep her silent. 'You know that's the truth, don't you? Tiffany's performing, just as she always performs. It's so much a part of her that she doesn't even know when she's doing it any more. She's looking death right in the eye, pretending that she isn't, and it's easy for her now, because it's just another performance. But pretty soon the truth is going to sink in, and it isn't going to be easy any more.' He closed his eyes briefly and sighed. 'There's no way they can restore power in time, Marnie. I think we both know that. And if I don't get some insulin up here, Tiffany is going to die. It's that simple. I'm not saying it's going to be easy, but I wouldn't like myself very much if I didn't try.'

Marnie choked back a sob, blinked rapidly, and felt tears tumble from both eyes.

'My God,' he murmured in amazement, wiping away the tears with his thumbs, 'which one of us do you care so much about? Tiffany, or me?'

Even if she had known what to answer, she wouldn't have had the chance, because he was kissing away the tears now, kissing first one eyelid, then the other, then her cheeks and the corner of her mouth, and just when the touch of his lips ceased to be comfort and changed into something else altogether, Tommy called out from upstairs.

'Ross? Marnie?'

Marnie pulled back like an embarrassed schoolgirl, but Ross grabbed her shoulders before she could turn away from him. He looked at her for a long moment before answering the voice at the top of the stairs.

'What is it, Tommy?'

The fashionable, useless hiking boots came down two steps, nearly tripped on the third, then moved more cautiously until Tommy stood half-way down the staircase. He ducked his head under the overhead beam to peer at them. 'It's darker than pitch down here,' he muttered, eyes unnaturally wide to catch the available light. 'I found another camping lantern upstairs if you want it.' His eyes found and focused on Marnie, and she felt the colour rise to her cheeks, as if he could tell what had happened down here just by looking at her.

Ross left her and took three steps over to the stairs. 'Another battery fluorescent?'

Tommy nodded.

'Keep it up there. I'll need it for the hike down. There's enough light for what I have to do down here already. Anything else?'

Tommy looked down quickly, then up again, nodding. 'Tiffany. She looked outside, and damn near fell apart. I don't think she'd guessed how bad the conditions were. She's almost hysterical, Ross. She doesn't think you should go. Frankly, neither do I,' he added in a low tone.

'Someone has to go, Tommy. We don't have a choice about that.'

'I know that. I just think the someone should be me. It's my fault this happened in the first place.'

Marnie's jaw dropped involuntarily. Tommy, pathetic, scrawny, almost effete Tommy, just wasn't cut out to be a hero. It was obviously never a role he aspired to, and she understood what the gesture had cost him. She was dumbfounded that he'd made it at all, but the night was full of surprises. Who would have thought that Tiffany would try to talk Ross out of going, when her own life depended on it? Everyone was acting out of character.

'Tommy,' Ross said quietly, 'the idea isn't to make a human sacrifice. The idea is to send the person most likely to get down and back. There's no shame in being out of your element here. This is no test of manhood, no macho scene. I just happen to be comfortable in the mountains, and you aren't, that's all. It doesn't make sense for you to go. Now if we were in Manhattan, you'd be the one I'd send down to the drugstore after dark. No way I'd take a risk like that. Understand?'

He'd said exactly the right thing, and Marnie was proud of him.

'I understand,' Tommy said, but the gratitude on his face was because Ross had understood. 'But she's making quite a scene up there. I don't think she'll let you go.'

'Then your work's cut out for you, Tommy. You'll have to convince her that it isn't as bad as it looks, that it's a piece of cake for an old hiker like me. I don't know much about diabetes, but I'd guess that it isn't helping her condition to be upset right now.'

'I'll do my best.' Tommy flashed a determined smile, then disappeared up the stairs.

'But it isn't "a piece of cake",' Marnie said quietly. 'You said yourself it wouldn't be easy—that probably means it's suicidal.'

Ross chuckled and pretended to scan the boxes on the floor. 'I'm ashamed to admit that I liked the idea of you worrying about me,' he said lightly. 'So I couldn't resist exaggerating the danger. I told you, Marnie, I know these mountains in winter. I'll be just fine.'

'Ross?'

He turned slowly and Marnie moved close enough to see the deep blue determination in his eyes that somehow belied his cocky smile. 'Tell me the truth.'

He shrugged impatiently. 'I'm telling you the truth. Buzz mentioned a public hiking trail that zigzags from the summit down to the base station. I told him I'd walk it one day. I'll bet he didn't think it would be this soon.' He sobered at her expression. 'It's a clearly marked trail, climbers use it all summer long. It's not like I'll have to rappel down a cliff or anything.'

'I think the operative words here are "all summer",' she said flatly, 'and you're insulting my intelligence. I know what blizzards are like, even on flat ground.'

'It's not going to be that bad, Marnie, but I'm not getting the job done standing here.' He rubbed his hands together briskly. 'Now, help me look for some rope, and any extra clothing you can find.'

The seed germinated while she was rummaging through a lost-and-found box. It took root in her mind as she sorted through mittens without mates, mismatched legwarmers, and half a dozen wool scarves. By the time she'd collected a considerable pile of usable items, her mind was made up.

'There,' she said, straightening from her squat, brushing her hands on her knees. 'That should help, don't you think?'

Ross looked at the towering pile of wool and laughed. 'Good grief, Marnie. I couldn't move if I wore all that. It's too much.'

'Not for the two of us,' she said quietly, looking straight at him.

He sucked in a quick breath, then blew it out in a single word. 'No.'

'Yes.'

'No. Absolutely not.' He dismissed the subject by turning away, so she made her accusation to his back.

'You told Tommy this wasn't a macho scene.'

'And it isn't! Sexual roles have nothing to do with it!'

'Oh, no? Then give me one good reason why I

shouldn't go with you.'

'Because it's stupid to risk two lives!' he shouted, spinning to face her. 'Because it *isn't* a piece of cake out there, and anything could happen on the way down. You could trip, break a leg, sprain an ankle . . .'

'And so could you,' she pointed out reasonably. 'And then where would Tiffany be? Where would you be, for that matter? But if two of us go, and something happened to one, at least there'd be a back-up.'

Ross glared at her as if this were war and she were the enemy. She could hear the effort as he struggled to keep his voice calm. 'The chances of my slipping up are minimal. I'm used to winter, and I'm used to the mountains. You don't have the first idea of what it's really like out there. You'd be frozen within minutes. You'd only slow me down, Marnie.' This last was spoken almost apologetically.

'You seem to forget that I'm the one with the snowmobile suit,' she said, keeping a rein on her temper, 'and the boots, and the mittens, and even a ski mask that fits.' Triumphantly, she plucked a woollen mask from the pile of lost-and-found. 'If you really believe that only one person should go, I'm the logical choice. I'm the only one dressed for the occasion.'

'Don't be ridiculous.'

'And I won't slow you down. I told you, I'm a country girl, born and raised.'

'You're a city transplant. You went soft long ago.'

'The hell I did!' She ground the mask into a soft ball and threw it at him. He just laughed and batted it away, then stopped suddenly and stared at her, eyes narrowed.

'You want to be the hero, don't you, Marnie?' he said quietly. 'You want to take charge, just as you always do, and fix everything. Well, this is one time that someone else is better suited to the job, so you might as well give it up and step aside. You want to help? Fine. Look for things I can use, and for God's sake, don't count yourself among them.' He turned away and busied himself with a length of rope.

Marnie just stood there, stunned to silence by his words, thinking that part of what he said was probably true, but part of it wasn't. She didn't want to be a hero or a person who took charge, or even a peacemaker. She'd never wanted to be any of those things. The role had just been thrust upon her, a long time ago.

For the moment, the only thing she really wanted was to keep one more man from walking out into a blizzard alone. And that she could do.

CHAPTER SEVEN

WITHIN half an hour Ross was rechecking the contents of a salvaged backpack for the third time—waterproof tins of wooden matches, spare mittens, socks, scarves, and a collection of high-energy dried food packets the restaurant stocked for summer hikers. His slimline thirty-five-millimetre camera hung around his neck, pressed against his chest by the weight of several sweaters. He was first and foremost a photographer, and going anywhere without at least one camera was unthinkable.

Marnie stood off to one side, calmly observing him in the dim light of the basement. She was terribly appealing to Ross at that moment with her short hair tousled, a smudge of dirt darkening her chin, and her brown eyes steady in that quiet, unreadable gaze of hers.

He rubbed at the black, scratchy stubble on his jaw and smiled at her. She'd been a tremendous help, actually, once she'd given up that ridiculous notion of tagging along. Not that he wouldn't have liked the company, but she wouldn't have been that. She would only have been something else for him to worry about, and that was a luxury he couldn't afford on this trip. Oh, she was capable enough when it came to handling the tantrums of temperamental models, but that was a far cry from making a mountain descent in a full-scale blizzard. Still, she was just stubborn enough to think she could do it, and he felt a peculiar satisfaction at having saved her from her own foolhardiness.

She returned his smile unexpectedly, and for a moment—just for one moment—he was tempted to relent and take her along. For one thing, she'd been right about safety in numbers. It would have been much more sensible for two to make the trek down the mountain. But then his eyes flicked over the woman's body, the soft hands, the delicate face, and his resolve strengthened. She might be tough enough in the narrow confines of her own world, independent enough within the protective security of familiar surroundings—but take those away and she'd be just as lost and helpless as Tommy without a credit card, or Tiffany and Bett without their mirrors. If anything, Marnie Weston would be worse than any of the rest in this particular situation, simply because she was afraid of the storm, and afraid of heights. He'd seen that in her face the moment she had stepped off the gondola.

'Are you ready?'

He hadn't realised how quiet they'd been until she spoke.

'As ready as I can be, under the circumstances.' He bent from the waist to check the laces on his boots, snapping the elastic of the long wool legwarmers over the leather tops.

'Those won't keep the snow from soaking through to your pants, you know.' She gestured at the navy blue wool that encased his legs from boot to mid-thigh.

'I know that, but since they're all I've got, they'll have to do. They'll keep some of the warmth in, anyway, and I'll dry them out at rest stops, if I can find a place to build a fire.'

She looked up at him and blinked, and the quiet determination in her gaze made him wonder again why she'd given in so easily. He'd been a little disappointed by that. For a while, she'd exhibited a fiery strength of purpose that had almost been admirable.

He shook his head as if to clear it from such thoughts, sending his black hair tumbling over his forehead. That strength would crumble, he reminded himself. Five minutes outside in these conditions and even a woman as strong as Marnie seemed to be would be overwhelmed.

'I'm ready,' he said suddenly, turning for the stairs. 'Bring the rope, will you?'

Marnie glanced down at the tangle of yellow nylon at her feet. 'Just as soon as I get it coiled. Go on up. I'll follow in a minute.'

The noise upstairs was a gruesome reminder of the storm raging outside. In the buried box of the basement where it was eerily silent, Ross had almost forgotten what he was preparing for. The stinging hiss of snow hitting the windows and the howl of wind in the chimney reminded him immediately.

Bett laughed as he approached the light given off by the fireplace. There was certainly nothing funny about the situation, but his appearance was comical, and they all needed the tension release of a good laugh.

'Not your average fashion-plate, am I?' Ross grinned, encouraging the comedy by turning to show off his outfit.

Even Tiffany raised herself listlessly on one elbow, looked at him, then giggled.

Good, he thought. Let her laugh. Let her think it's a lark, and maybe then she won't realise how slim my chances of getting back in time really are.

'Cute, huh?' he clowned deliberately, then pretended offence at their laughter.

The lost-and-found box had been a godsend. He wore two brightly patterned sweaters over his own under the ski jacket, and over all of this he had wound a blanket that fell to his hips. Another was threaded through his legs, around each thigh to cover those parts the legwarmers missed, and up to tie at the waist. He was totally encased in a maze of different fabrics and colours, and felt a little like he had been wrapped for an Egyptian burial.

'Fold another blanket as small as you can for the backpack, Tommy, will you? And, Bett, put some hot coffee in one of those little Thermos flasks. You'll find them under the sink.'

While they rushed to do his bidding, he walked over to where Tiffany lay, looking incredibly beautiful, and incredibly pale. 'And your job is to rest,' he smiled down at her. 'It's going to take all night to get down there, but I'll be back with some of that magic stuff you're hooked on before noon tomorrow. Soon enough?'

She nodded slowly, her lower lip quivering.

'What do I ask for, by the way?' He coaxed a smile out of her to forestall the tears. 'A six-pack of insulin, please, or one gallon to go?'

'I wrote it down.' She handed him a napkin with unintelligible words scribbled on it. 'Any pharmacist will know what I need from that.'

He looked down to unzip the chest pocket of his jacket, tucked the folded napkin into the plastic-lined compartment, then zipped it closed.

'I had every intention of doing everything I could to stop you,' Tiffany said. 'Until this very moment, I didn't believe it when Tommy said it wasn't dangerous.'

Ross cocked one brow. 'Until this moment? What finally convinced you?'

She nodded to a point behind him and smiled, the first totally genuine smile he'd seen from her since she'd discovered her bag was missing. 'Because you wouldn't take Marnie with you if it were at all dangerous. I feel a lot better about things now. For the first time, I think I actually may survive this mess.'

Ross's smile froze as he turned slowly in place. Marnie stood just behind him, her snowmobile suit obscured by her own collection of mismatched garments. Her smile was triumphant and infuriatingly smug.

She had him. Damn her for her foolishness, she had him. There was no way he could repeat his objections without alarming Tiffany, and one look at the healthy brightening of her expression after seeing Marnie made it perfectly clear that her state of mind was critical. He didn't dare say a thing.

'Tommy didn't tell me you were going along, Marnie,' Tiffany said from behind him; and indeed, Tommy hadn't. Even now he was half bent over a tightly folded blanket, staring at Marnie in slack-jawed disbelief.

Marnie moved next to Ross and shrugged impishly down at Tiffany. 'Surely you didn't expect me to pass up a chance like this? Alone in the wilderness with Ross Arnett for a whole night? I'll be the envy of every woman I know.'

Tiffany actually giggled, but Ross couldn't trust himself to speak, he was so enraged. Marnie's flip comments made the whole thing sound like some adolescent outing, some adventurous field trip with no more potential for danger than a trip to the local museum. That was all very well for Tiffany to believe, but he and Marnie both knew better what waited out there.

She smiled up at him, a little smugly, but her smile faltered when his gaze came to cold, quiet rest on her face. All right, Marnie Weston, he thought, a disturbing smile tugging at one side of his mouth. You tricked me, you won, and you're feeling pretty superior about it. But the joke's on you. Let's see how superior you feel once we're outside. Let's see how you like your little victory when frostbite deadens the nerves in your face and you can't feel your feet any more.

His smile broadened darkly as he relished the thought of Marnie's finally being forced to admit that he was right all along. God knew, he'd tried to spare her the ordeal that was surely to come, but she wouldn't listen, and now she was going to pay for that. He could hardly wait for her first pathetic, whining complaint. It probably wouldn't take long; maybe just a few minutes out in the blizzard, and then he'd send her back inside and proceed on his own. And, even as he anticipated the pleasure of his revenge, a part of him wished she could be spared that ultimate humiliation.

Marnie watched Ross warily, as she would have watched a driverless car careening down a road, ready to jump clear if it suddenly veered in her direction. Let the others laugh at his clownish attire and the light-hearted feeling they were trying to impart; all she had to do was look into those eyes to know there was absolutely nothing funny about what he was feeling right now.

She shifted uncomfortably under his stare. So what if it had been a little deceptive, the way she'd trapped him into taking her along? It was for his own good, after all. It wasn't as if she'd been trying to beat him in some silly male-female competition.

'All right, Marnie,' Ross interrupted her thoughts.

'Yes?' Her reply was too quick, too loud, like a gunshot.

Ross frowned at her uncertainly, a little surprised by the high tension in her tone. 'We'd better get started.'

After some last-minute adjustments of scarves and backpacks, Marnie and Ross were poised at the door, two sexless bipeds of indeterminate features beneath their bulky wrappings.

'Don't push me off the top of this mountain,' Marnie said to him in a quick aside. 'It's safer with two of us. I had to come along.'

Ross just glared at her as he wound a heavy scarf around his face until all that remained uncovered was a slit for his eyes. Marnie pulled the black ski mask over her head and adjusted it until she could look out through the two round openings in the wool. Another slash in the mask left her lips exposed, but the rest of her face was completely covered.

Calls of good luck and, preposterously, Bett's admonition to 'have fun', were lost to the howl of the wind as they opened the door and stepped out into the night.

Nothing had prepared Marnie for the horror just outside the glass walls. Wind-driven snow, heavier than anything she had seen in her life, reduced visibility to less than a foot. She had gasped at the first icy kiss of the frigid air, felt the sharp pain deep in her lungs, and recalled instantly a lesson she had learned as a child during winters on the Midwestern plains. Shallow breaths only, through your nose, so the air warms in your sinus cavity before travelling down to the lungs. It wasn't merely a precaution for comfort; it was a matter of life and death, because lung tissue could freeze easily.

She stood still for a moment, eyes closed, trying to regulate her breathing. Her body wanted to respond to the thin, oxygen-poor air with deep breaths, and she had to fight that instinct to survive. For a few seconds she panicked, imagining that she would suffocate under the claustrophobic pressure of the mask over her nose, but eventually she was calm enough to open her eyes. When she held her hand out at arm's length it disappeared in a curtain of swirling snow, and she felt the pincers of justifiable fear deep in her stomach. Dear God! She was enveloped by a mad swirl of white, and beyond that there was nothing but absolute darkness. The world was gone.

Suddenly she was frozen where she stood—not yet by the cold—it would be some time before that penetrated her shield of insulation—but by sheer terror. Had it been this bad for Jimmy? Her mind sent frantic messages along innumerable neurons to her feet, commanding that they move forward, and yet they refused. Was Ross there? They were only just outside the door, less than a foot from the building behind them, and yet she had no sense at all of his presence. Had he left her behind? Was he on his way down the mountain already, while she stood here alone?

Even this close to the building, the thought of being left alone terrified her more than the conditions, and she spurted forward in two quick, panicked steps. A mittened hand shot from the billowing curtain of white and grabbed her arm. She jumped away in alarm, then relaxed a little when Ross pulled her close enough to look up and see him.

They each carried one of the battery-powered camping lights, and he tilted his to shine up on his face. The cone of light made his head appear suspended in the swirling snow, disembodied, but it reflected in the deep blue of his eyes, and at that moment his eyes were eloquent. Even narrowed to protective slits against the snow and wind, Marnie could see the challenge in them, and the question. He was feeding on her fear, counting on it, waiting for her to turn away from the test and go back to the safety inside.

Their eyes waged silent war for only an instant, then Marnie nodded once, very firmly, and gestured for Ross to lead the way. She saw a flicker of surprise in his eyes, and smiled beneath her ski mask as he turned and stepped away from her into the drifted snow.

Back in the restaurant, Ross had tied them together at the waist, with only a few feet of the nylon rope slack between them. The moment he moved away from her, she understood why. With only one step, he disappeared into the wall of snow. Only the taut rope at her waist reminded her that she was not alone. She stumbled at the first tug, and only just managed to regain her balance before falling headfirst into the snow. A fall this early would be disastrous, she knew, coating her with wet snow, sapping valuable warmth from her body.

Pay attention, keep up the pace, don't fall, don't slow him down. Even though she knew her leg muscles would protest in agony later, she struggled to follow quickly enough to keep the rope between them slack.

In point of fact, even though Marnie was pushing herself to the limit to keep up, Ross was moving slower than he would have liked. The snow was already knee-high between the drifts, and breaking a path through it was slow-going. At least it was still soft enough to plough through, thank God. When the temperatures started to plummet on the lee side of the low-pressure system that had given birth to the blizzard, the snow's exposed surfaces would freeze into a brittle crust. Then the option of pushing through the white stuff would be gone, and a hiker would be forced to lift one heavy boot high, plunge through the crust up to the thigh, lift the other boot, and repeat the procedure endlessly. That particular struggle for progress would be quickly exhausting, and would burn heat-producing calories at an alarming rate. For now, Ross was grateful that he could use his legs as a crude plough. That he blazed an easier trail for Marnie in the process was unintentional.

With dogged determination, Ross pushed his way across the snow-covered deck surrounding the restaurant until they were in the shelter of the building's east side. Amazingly, there was very little new snow here, and very little wind. The first of the bright orange signs that marked the hiking trail loomed directly ahead. In full daylight, it looked as if the sign was poised over the brink of nothingness; tonight, in the glow of Ross's lantern, it appeared to be standing in front of a solid white curtain. He parted the scarf over his mouth and spoke close to Marnie's covered ear.

'The trail starts here, and for the first few hundred yards, it should be pretty easy going. On this side of the face, the winds won't be so bad, but the further we head west, the worse it will get. Be ready for it.'

Marnie felt her eyes widen with anxiety, then

squinted quickly against the drying effect of the cold. 'But you said it was only this bad at the top,' she reminded him.

His shoulders moved under the blanket, already sporting a layer of heavy snow. 'I lied.'

She closed her eyes in dismay. So far they'd only walked from the front of the building to the side, already she was exhausted, and now he was telling her that she hadn't seen anything yet.

Ross saw the slight slump to her shoulders, the closed eyes, but felt no satisfaction in seeing her fear. Whatever else she was, she was a brave woman, and bravery deserved better than humiliation.

'Go back, Marnie,' he told her tenderly. 'It's going to be bad.'

Her eyes flashed open. 'I know that. That's why I came along in the first place, and I won't go back.'

'Marnie,' he said through clenched teeth, 'I don't want you out in this . . .'

'And I don't want *you* out in this!' she fired back without thinking, then dropped her head, embarrassed.

Ross saw the irony that never even occurred to Marnie. Here they were, two stubborn people, screaming in the middle of a blizzard on top of a mountain, each trying desperately to protect the other. He didn't know where the feelings had come from, but the startling realisation that they were there made him smile a little beneath his scarf. 'OK, Marnie. We'd better get started.'

'I'm ready,' she said with false confidence, but dread was already settling in the back of her mind, as black as the world beyond the visible shroud of snow. She steeled herself for what was to come and prepared to follow a man she barely knew into the unknown.

In the height of the summer season, the trail's only challenges came at the end of each ramp where there was a sharper descent for a few yards before it switched back to cross in the other direction. But that was in the summer, and the very provisions that made the hike comfortable at that time of year worked against Ross and Marnie now.

The openness of the path, permitting impressive photographs in dry weather, became calamitous during the snowy months. Above the tree line on the western side of the face, there was absolutely no cover. Driven snow piled high on the trail and sloped dangerously to bank on the sheer wall behind it.

Had Ross anticipated that this was what lay ahead, he would have bound and gagged Marnie back in the basement to keep her from coming along. As it was, he didn't find out until it was much too late.

CHAPTER EIGHT

THE TREK downward began easily, just as Ross had promised. On the eastern side of the mountain face they were sheltered somewhat from the wind and snow, and Marnie followed Ross almost happily.

Once off the summit itself, the visibility was so improved that she could easily see not only the rope and Ross, but the beam of his lantern lighting the way ahead. It was dark, it was cold, and it was certainly snowing; but the footing was sure, and the wind was no longer so strong that it drowned out their voices.

'Don't use your light unless you absolutely have to,' Ross called over his shoulder. 'I don't know how long these batteries will last in this cold, and we'll need it later. Just follow my footsteps. I promise not to lead you off the edge.'

'No problem,' she called ahead. 'I can see your light just fine. And, Ross, you were right. It *is* a piece of cake.'

She saw him shake his head, but he made no comment.

They plodded steadily down the gradual slope toward the west, Marnie happily oblivious, Ross squinting furiously into the darkness beyond the range of his light. He was alert for a gradual increase in wind, but when it came it was so sudden that it took him by surprise.

They had just rounded a bulge in the mountain's side, one they would later learn ran from the top to the bottom like a crooked spine. The bulge shielded the eastern side of the face from the wind, and conditions were tolerable there, but on the west it was a nightmare.

The first gust of wind hit Ross with such force that his arms flew outward for balance as he was shoved backwards toward Marnie. She saw him coming soon enough to brace herself against the impact, but without his body as a windbreak she was even more helpless than he was. Instinctively, she sat down hard in her own footprints, making a smaller target with a more stable base. Involuntarily, Ross followed suit as the rope connecting them jerked him down. He ended up sitting between Marnie's outspread legs, his back pressed against her chest. The ludicrous thought that they looked like they were riding double on a non-existent motorcycle popped into Marnie's head.

'Now the fun starts!' Ross shouted through his scarves, scrambling to get up before the snow soaked through his clothes.

Marnie just sat there while the rope pulled at her waist, trying to catch her breath.

'Get up, dammit!' he shouted down at her. 'Get up before it buries you!'

She snapped to a sudden, horrifying awareness that such a thing could easily happen, and staggered to her feet. She'd been down for only seconds, yet the snow had completely covered her legs in that time.

Actually, it was hard to think of it as snow at

all. What was falling bore little resemblance to those intricately patterned shapes schoolchildren cut from white paper. It looked more like a solid wall than a collection of individual flakes, and what was even more disconcerting, it didn't seem to be falling from the sky. The wind was driving it straight toward them, parallel to the ground.

Oh, lord, Marnie murmured in her mind, because speech was utterly impossible. Every time she opened her mouth the wind drove snow and cold down her throat. She wanted to shout that they couldn't possibly go on, that mere humans were no match for this particular brand of nature's violence, but she was helpless to do even that. She had no choice but to follow the determined figure ploughing his way through the drifts ahead, tugging her mercilessly along behind him.

They bent against the wind, their bodies tilted at impossible angles to the ground, their heads down and to the side for what meagre protection that allowed. After the first few steps Marnie's vision became blurred, and she blinked repeatedly, trying to clear it. Eventually she realised that her eyelashes had become coated and frozen, and that blurred vision was something she'd better get used to. It would be with her all the way down the mountain, or until she dropped from exhaustion—whichever came first.

How much worse it must be for Ross, she thought, ploughing a path with his legs, open to the full force of the wind without even the shield of another body in front of him. She held that thought as her face grew numb, then her hands, then her feet. Neither mask nor mittens nor boots were protection enough against the swirling cold.

Time held no meaning as the two snow-covered figures, dwarfed by the mountain's fearsome majesty, made their way across the face into the ever-worsening storm. Every step was a hard-fought battle, won at great cost, and served only to take them further and further into the nightmarish web of the blizzard's core.

At first Marnie occupied her mind by anticipating the rest stop that must certainly come soon. Maybe one more step, she told herself, maybe two, and then he'll stop and you can sit down, your back to the wind. Eventually she stopped dreaming of rest because it distracted her from the painful process of taking one step forward, then another, and still another. Her mind now as numb as her body, it was impossible to spare a single thought for anything other than the grindingly slow, exhausting progress forward.

Just ahead of her, lost in a swirl of snow, Ross moved with machine-like steadiness through the drifts, faintly surprised that his legs still obeyed the automatic commands of his mind. That first fall had been a costly one. In spite of the speed with which he had regained his feet, the wet snow had soaked through the legwarmers, and he now had only a slight sensation of feeling below his knees. He knew they would have to stop soon, but he also knew that he didn't dare until he could build a fire to dry out his clothing. On this side of the mountain's spine, the wind made a fire impossible. They had to make the first switchback, then follow the trail back past the bulge, to the eastern side of the face before they could hope to find shelter. He knew he could make it; he had to. His life depended on it, or at the very least, his legs. But Marnie was another matter.

By God, he thought, she had been a trooper up to now. Never flagging, never complaining, although to be perfectly fair it was impossible to complain when you couldn't open your mouth. Still, she had stayed with him every step of the way, and when he remembered her obvious fear of both heights and the storm, he felt the unusual poignancy of genuine admiration. Grudgingly, he had to admit it: Marnie Weston was stronger than he had thought. At least, she had been. Lately, over the past fifty yards or so, he'd felt momentary resistance on the rope whenever he took a step. It was obvious that exhaustion was taking its toll, slowing her down. She needed a rest, perhaps more than he did. Unfortunately, he couldn't afford to give it to her. He'd seen the creeping black of frostbite on other men's limbs, and he had no desire to see it on his own. No matter how badly they both needed it, not even if she should beg for it, he could not, would not stop until they found shelter for a fire.

Ross's mechanical movements forward were so mindless that he barely took note of the first switchback in the trail when they reached it. One minute he was pushing through snow piled over his knees, the next minute the trail dropped suddenly beneath his feet. He paused only long enough to shine his light downward, assessing the trail.

It wasn't a particularly difficult descent. Large

boulders jutted out from the rock wall, almost like steps, but the wind had swept them free of snow, leaving a slick coating of ice beneath. He went down to a sitting position, gestured for Marnie to do the same, and they went down on their seats like toddling children on a staircase. At the bottom they found the trail again, leading back the way they had come, and gradually downward. With the wind at their backs now, they plodded down the gentle slope without a moment's rest.

It no longer occurred to Marnie that she was tired. Being simply tired was a vaguely pleasant memory from the distant past. There wasn't a word in the language to describe the agonising exhaustion she felt now. But neither did it occur to her to plead for a rest. Ross was going forward, ever forward, and some primitive sense demanded that she follow him without question. In a corner of her mind that clung stubbornly to the belief that men and women were equal in all things, her own meekness troubled her. She'd always found the man-shall-lead-and-woman-shall-follow school of thought distasteful, and she couldn't understand why she wasn't filing a vehement protest.

I'm going to tell him we have to stop and rest, she'd think with determination, but in the next instant some deeper, more primitive instinct would prevail, and she would hold her tongue and continue to follow, playing out a role as ancient and established as humanity itself.

It was easier to make out his dark shape with the wind at their backs. The light from his lantern bounced back from the curtain of snow ahead, and although she tried to focus on that her eyes kept drifting back to the man who led her.

The blanket that had been so carefully wound around his thighs flapped wildly now, and his back was completely encrusted with snow. She imagined that her own back must look the same; that together they probably looked like two barely mobile snowmen, brought to horrible life by the storm.

Existence had been reduced to an endless equation of single steps. Marnie concentrated on one at a time, never thinking about anything as far in the future as the next one. The secret to endurance was to concentrate on the immediate. Lift one knee high, let the wind push your body forward, then plant the foot. Simple. Child's play. And yet the sense of achievement after successfully completing each step was enormous. The wind pushed against her back like an unrelenting hand, and even if she had tried to stop it would have shoved her onward.

Ross rounded the telltale bulge of the mountain's spine and stepped into the relative calm on the other side. For the first time in what seemed like years, he could see clearly what lay ahead for the unimaginable distance of five feet or so. He stopped dead in the middle of the trail and let his arms hang limply at his sides. Marnie came up next to him.

'Now what?' she shouted, but the wind was still strong enough to blow her words away.

Ross squinted down at her through frozen lashes, shook his head in mute exhaustion, then stumbled forward again.

They struggled almost to the end of the ramp before they found the shelter, and even then it was sheer providence that they discovered it at all. Ross had stumbled on legs he could no longer feel and his lantern had fallen to the snow, its weak glow pointing to a dark opening in the face of the mountain. He dropped to his knees and crawled in, turned his head to make sure Marnie was right behind him, then his legs gave way and he crumpled on top of the lantern. He wanted to say something clever, something reassuring as his head touched the cold rock floor, but his lips were too stiff to form words. For the moment, all he could do was savour the sudden, blessed quiet.

The moment he collapsed on the lantern, Marnie was plunged into total, terrifying darkness. She sucked in an alarmed breath and went rigid, poised on hands and knees like a startled deer. 'Ross?' she whispered, but there was no answer. She could hear the faint howl of the wind just outside, but within the shelter it was almost frighteningly quiet. The only breathing she could hear was her own. She could actually feel her pupils enlarge to admit any available light, but there simply wasn't any. Only blackness. 'Dammit, Ross, answer me!'

She waved her right arm in a blind arc in front of her, and felt the stiff tangle of blankets just ahead. Finally remembering her own lantern, she switched it on, and cast its light on the inert figure before her.

'Oh, my God,' she murmured, her own panic forgotten at the sight of him.

He lay crumpled on his side, just inside the shallow depression that had been carved into the mountain's face eons ago. The scarf had slipped from his face, and Marnie saw the deathly white skin stretched over his cheekbones that preceded imminent frostbite. Frozen white strands poked from under his black knit cap, and his lashes were a thick curtain of frost lying against his cheeks. His legs were positioned awkwardly under his body, and when she ripped off her mitten to adjust them, his thin trousers crackled, long since soaked and frozen into solidity.

His eyes opened to slits, slammed shut against the light, and then, incredibly, his white lips curved in a stiff smile that was more ghastly than reassuring. Marnie's shoulders sagged with relief.

'Look at you,' she grumbled, her words distorted by the frozen wool of her ski mask. 'Why didn't you stop? Why didn't you tell me you were soaked through? You could have killed yourself out there, you know that?'

He just shook his head tiredly and got to his knees to push past her.

'Where do you think you're going?' she said quickly.

'To get wood,' he said, his lips too numb to elaborate.

'You stay here,' she commanded, scrambling to get past him out the narrowing opening. 'I'll go.'

'No.'

She looked at him in utter disbelief, but the effectiveness of her expression was lost beneath the cover of her ski mask. 'Don't start *that* again. What is this thing you have about women carrying firewood, anyway?'

He'd been holding his lips pressed together to warm them, his eyes closed as if she were trying his patience intolerably. 'I don't know how far it is to the tree-line,' he said, barely able to enunciate. 'I can carry more in one trip than you can.'

Marnie's eyes flashed furiously. 'I can make two trips if I have to,' she snapped. 'I'm the one who's dressed for it. Look at you. Your trousers are already frozen stiff. Now you just stay where you are and . . .'

She hadn't been expecting the firm, surprisingly strong push that knocked her to her seat, and the air left her lungs with a startled whooshing sound. 'You're staying right here,' he commanded.

'What is this?' she snapped at him, furious. 'You mighty hunter, me weak woman?'

'Something like that,' he mumbled.

'You can't go out there!' she shouted, desperation making her blurt out her worst fear. 'You could die out there alone!'

Ross ignored her and began to shed the constricting tangle of blanket around his thighs.

'All right, then!' she huffed, gaining her knees again, backing out of the opening. 'We'll both go. Two can carry more wood than one, anyway.'

'No!' His hand snaked out and grabbed her arm, dragging her back inside. One firm jerk brought her eyes to within inches of his. 'Look at us, Marnie,' he hissed urgently. 'Don't you understand? We'll both freeze in here if we don't stop fighting about which one of us is going to take care of the other.'

Her face sagged a little. Was that what they were doing?

Preposterously, his eyes crinkled in a mischievous smile. 'Besides, I'd win in the end anyway. I'm stronger.' He poked one finger at his chest. 'Mighty hunter, remember?'

And so, for the second time in her life, Marnie stayed behind while someone else disappeared into the white-flecked darkness of a wintry night. She knelt quietly in the entryway of the shelter, fearful eyes trained on that spot where she had seen him last, wondering if this one, too, would never come back.

He was gone for ever. She'd checked her watch when he left, and even though she knew only fifteen minutes had passed by the time he stumbled back up the trail, it had still been for ever. She released a small sigh of relief. At least now she could quit worrying about him and just be angry that he had made her worry in the first place.

He dropped a motley collection of pine twigs and long, gnarled branches just outside, then crawled slowly through the opening. She gasped when she saw the deathly pallor of his face in the glow of the lantern.

'Guess what?' His grin was a pained pretence. 'We're just a little way from the next switchback. The tree-line starts at the bottom of that. Not so far to go for wood, after all.' He paused, looked at her expression, then chuckled. The anger almost hid the relief, but not quite.

'Oh, Marnie,' he teased gently. 'You shouldn't worry about me so much. A man could learn to like that.'

'I'd worry about *anyone* stupid enough to go out

alone in this weather!' she shot back.

'Maybe,' he smiled, 'but not as much as you worried about me.'

Before she could think of a snappy retort he had bent to strip off his trousers and legwarmers, and for some reason she found that very distracting.

'Well, what are you waiting for?' He smiled without looking up from his task. 'You were so anxious to do something, so go build a fire. I'll pose for you later, if you like. You can look at my legs all you want then.'

Marnie sucked in a breath and felt her face go hot. 'I was not looking at your legs!'

'Ah, but you were,' he grinned, 'and that's perfectly all right with me, as long as I get equal time later.'

'I was *not* looking at your legs!'

He wanted to laugh at the indignant protest, but he was too tired. 'Go on, Marnie. Start the fire.'

'I'll start the damn fire when you stop giving me orders!'

He grinned painfully at the stubborn jut of her chin. She looked like a ten-year-old on the verge of a tantrum. 'Marnie, Marnie,' he sighed, shaking his head. 'Such a temper. Now go on. Fire-building is a noble, manly task. You won't lose your feminist standing, I promise.'

She blew out a furious exhale and scrambled outside to hunch over the pile of wood. God, if she had to die on top of a mountain with someone, why did it have to be an oversexed man who thought he was the answer to every woman's prayers?

CHAPTER NINE

ROSS woke instantly, his mind racing even before he opened his eyes, trying to assimilate the furious clatter of gunfire . . . gunfire? His eyes flew open at the same instant he started to jerk to a sitting position, but hands on his shoulders held him down.

'Careful.' He looked up at Marnie's face hovering over him, eerily lit by the glow of a nearby camping lamp. 'You sit up too fast in here and you'll crack your head wide open.' Her eyes lifted to the low ceiling.

'No doubt a pleasure you want reserved for yourself,' he said with a wry grin, easing back down, arms outstretched. 'Well, never let it be said that Ross Arnett tried to get up when a good woman was pushing him down.' He grinned. 'I surrender. Take me. I'm yours.'

Marnie frowned down at her hands on his shoulders, blushed furiously, then snatched them away, much to Ross's amusement. While she scrambled crab-like away from him, Ross braced himself on his elbows and took a cursory look at his surroundings.

It wasn't a cave, not really. Just a shallow depression in the rockface shaped like a bowl standing on its side. There was no more floor space than a double bed, and barely enough head-room to sit up straight, but it was totally protected from the wind, and small enough to preserve heat.

He glanced up at the fire crackling just outside the opening, sparks shooting up into a curtain of falling snow. Golden flames reflected in the blue of his eyes. He nodded with approval as the superheated pine needles crackled to life, igniting the twigs that would in turn set fire to the larger branches layered on top. So that had been the gunfire he'd imagined.

'How long was I asleep?'

She glanced at her watch. 'Less than ten minutes.' She was sitting cross-legged less than two feet away, her attention riveted on the hungry tongues of flame as she fed them more twigs.

'And did you have your way with me when I was helpless?' He was leaning back against the wall, arms crossed over his chest, a maddening grin slicing the dark shadow of his lower face.

'I wasn't tempted,' she replied smartly.

He was silent for a moment, and she was afraid to look at him. 'Then explain what happened between us in the basement.'

Marnie kept her eyes on the fire, and hoped he would mistake her blush as a reaction to the heat. 'Forget the basement.'

'Not a chance.'

The fire cracked an alarm as the first of the larger branches ignited, and a sudden rush of heat filled the tiny shelter. Ross started to pull off his jacket, his eyes on her flushed face. 'Get out of that snowmobile suit before you start to sweat,' he commanded.

She lifted her chin and looked down her short nose at him. 'I'll take it off when I'm ready,' she said spitefully.

For a moment there was no sound but for the distant whistle of wind outside, and the occasional crackle of the fire.

'Take the snowmobile suit off, Marnie.'

She spun her head and glared at him. 'I'm not warm enough yet.'

'Or I will.'

Her jaw dropped before she could control it, and she thought absently how odd it was that that particular muscle could be so relaxed, when every other one in her body had gone suddenly rigid.

'Don't think I won't.'

He was actually smiling, damn him, actually enjoying making her squirm, and suddenly she was very hot indeed.

She kept her eyes on him while her hand strayed to the zipper at the top of her suit.

'That's better.' He nodded, making her feel like a new puppy that had finally been housebroken. He started to pull off all but the black sweater that was his own. 'If you get too hot, you sweat; and if you sweat in this weather, you get chilled; and if you get chilled, your body uses more calories to produce heat . . .'

'And if I got very, very lucky that would kill me and I wouldn't have to listen to you lecture any more!'

He laughed out loud and leaned back, smiling at her across the narrow expanse as if she had performed exactly as expected, and he was very pleased with her. 'Astonishing,' he said, shaking his head. 'You have the most astonishing temper for someone with the title of peacemaker.'

Just hearing it stated aloud drained the anger from her. She was Marnie Weston, and Marnie Weston never wasted time or energy on petty displays of temper. They were counterproductive. She concentrated on her muscles, one by one, forcing them to relax, and gradually the fury subsided. She was back in control again. 'Don't call me that,' she said tonelessly.

She turned her head to look at the fire, and Ross bit down on the ready retort when the firelight caught her in profile. It was one of those moments, one of those rare, elusive moments he spent his life waiting for.

My God, he mused silently, his hands quietly, unobtrusively fumbling for his camera. Look at her.

He'd expected weakness, fear, even hysteria from this woman—from *any* woman faced with the conditions they'd had to endure—and instead she delivered this sudden, incredible picture of peace.

There was no mark of hardship on her face, no anxiety about what still lay ahead. Just something quietly determined about her expression as she gazed into the fire; something placid, and constant; a subtle, uniquely feminine strength, totally unlike the brute physical strength of a man, yet in its own way every bit as powerful. He imagined that the pioneer women of a century ago must have worn that same look as they gazed into campfires on their way west across the empty plains, and the thought took his breath away.

Quietly, carefully, he drew his camera from under

his sweater, adjusted the shutter speed, and snapped his first photograph.

'What are you doing?' Her head had snapped around at the click of the shutter.

'Saving the moment,' he said quietly, looking straight at her. 'That's what I do, you know. Catch moments, and save them for ever.'

She turned back to the fire, pretending indifference. 'Some moments aren't worth saving.'

'That one was,' he replied. He clicked the shutter again, catching her in profile.

'I can't believe you actually brought that thing along,' she said irritably, picturing her exhausted, unkempt image in his album of perfection.

'I take it everywhere.' He clicked the shutter again. 'Don't you like having your picture taken?'

'No.'

Click, click.

'Too bad. You're a great subject.'

'Please stop it,' she said coldly, turning her face away.

Click.

'I said stop it!'

He lifted the strap from around his neck and set the camera carefully to one side. 'The peacemaker is losing her temper again,' he said slyly.

Marnie sighed in exasperation, thinking how odd it was that the ridiculous title usually fitted; this was the only person in years who had managed to scratch the surface and find the temper beneath. He had the uncanny knack of bringing out what she had been taught was the worst in her—anger—and while con-

sciously that disturbed her, subconsciously there was
something pure, something cleansing about it that
made anger at Ross Arnett almost a pleasure.

'I told you to stop calling me that,' she said evenly.

He smiled at her. 'I have to admit it certainly
doesn't suit you. Where did you get such a ridiculous
label?'

'I earned it,' she said tiredly, staring into the
hypnotic flicker of the fire, remembering.

Her father's voice reverberated in her mind,
crossing the span of years and miles. 'I know it's hard,
Marnie, but you just can't lose your temper with
Jimmy. You have to be stronger than he is.'

She saw herself—lord, had she ever been so
small?—a girl of nine, with knobbly knees and dark
eyes too big for her face, tears at the ready, pouting up
at the god-face of her father. 'But, Daddy, he *hit* me.
He hits me all the time. Why can't I hit him back?'

'Because he's your little brother, Marnie, and he's
not as lucky as you are. He's mad at the world, and so
he strikes out at you, and that's when you have to be
especially strong. You can do that for me, Marnie,
can't you? It's easy to strike back, you know. Not
doing it is the hardest thing of all. Only the very, very
strong can do that. Blessed are the peacemakers,
Marnie. Remember that when Jimmy hits you again.
Now, can you give me your sacred promise that you
won't lose your temper any more?'

And Marnie had, because life had dealt Jimmy one
of those ghastly, tragic blows that aren't ever
supposed to happen. He was one of a handful of
children nationwide who were, in a cruel irony,

crippled by the very polio vaccine meant to spare them the disease. Something distorted about their immune system, something beyond the comprehension of even the scientists at the time, made a few children react to the vaccine by developing the disease itself, instead of antibodies against it. It happened so very rarely, the distraught doctors apologised to John and Ethel Weston. There were almost no cases on record. The chances of such a dreadful thing happening were a million to one . . . but that was small consolation when it was your child who was that one in a million.

Jimmy almost died. Then he lay motionless in bed for nearly a year, and then he staggered on braces and crutches for another year, a furious, frustrated seven-year-old who hit his sister because she could walk and he couldn't. After that fateful promise to her father, Marnie's only defence was to step out of range, and because she was nimble it maddened Jimmy beyond reason. It was during one of these black rages that he threw his crutches down in fury and took his first triumphant step without them, and that was the beginning. Jimmy never hit her again.

Within a year the crutches were gathering dust in the attic of the big white farmhouse. After another year, the braces joined them . . .

'Marnie?'

She flinched, then blinked.

'Marnie?'

'What?' She looked over at Ross, and for just an instant the pictures in her mind blurred with reality, crossing over into one another, and she saw something of Jimmy in Ross Arnett's eyes.

He frowned at the start of recognition he saw in her face, but it was gone almost before he could be sure it was ever there at all.

'I called your name four times.'

She just nodded, then looked back at the fire. He didn't look like Jimmy any more. Thank God. She felt the bulk of her discarded snowmobile suit behind her, and pushed it absently to one side.

Ross ran one hand back through his hair, frustrated by her solitary journey into thoughts he could not read. He was no longer tempted to take her picture. Sometimes the human face was too eloquent, and recording those expressions was an unforgivable intrusion. His thoughts floundered, searching for a safe subject.

'Now there's a contradiction for you,' he said lightly. 'A woman who hates winter with a snowmobile suit.'

'It's very old,' she said distantly, smiling a little. 'Jimmy and I used to spend most of the winter on snowmobiles. He used to scare me, going so fast I could hardly keep up.' She looked at Ross with a wistful smile. 'It was never fast enough for Jimmy.'

Ross nodded, perhaps remembering his own youth. 'The young boy's love-affair with speed. We all go through that, I think.'

'No,' she mused softly, shaking her head, staring at some far away point just behind Ross's head. She was silent for so long that he wasn't sure she was going to say anything else. 'It was more than that with Jimmy. He'd had polio when he was very young. I think that was why he loved speed so much. Even after he'd recovered, he could never seem to go fast enough. I suppose he was making up for all the lost time he'd spent in those braces.'

Ross was silent for a moment. 'Your brother had polio?'

'When he was five.' Her expression sobered. 'He had a very hard time of it. We couldn't do the things the other children did, of course, and the frustration was terrible for him.'

The 'we' hadn't been lost on Ross. 'How old were you then?' he asked carefully.

She frowned and tipped her head, thinking. 'Seven, when he got it. We were both teenagers by the time he'd completely recovered.'

Ross sucked air in through his teeth. Suddenly he had a very clear picture of what Marnie's childhood had been like. He saw a solemn young girl, constant, protective companion to her crippled brother, forced too soon into a role of awesome responsibility, learning early to repress anger, impatience, impulsiveness—all the natural emotions of childhood.

He stirred with the need to put his arms around her, to take care of that little girl who had always taken care of someone else, and realised that this was something he had wanted to do since he'd first seen her pop out of the gondola, pale, clearly shaken, yet somehow stoic. Ross had wanted many women in his lifetime, but this was the first time he had wanted to take *care* of one, and the feeling confused him. The irony was almost laughable. The truly dependent women, the insecure Tiffanys and Betts of the world, had never inspired the strange protective instincts Marnie seemed to bring to the fore. She was the first, and she was too self-sufficient to ever make use of them.

Marnie was watching his face carefully, measuring the physical evidence of sympathy she thought he was feeling for Jimmy. 'I don't know why I told you all that,' she said with a nervous smile.

Ross leaned back against the wall while he looked at her. Individual strands of her short hair stood away from her head in a dark halo, electrified by the dry heat. She pushed her fingers back through it in a nervous gesture, frowning at the muted crackle of static, wondering why he was so silent, why he kept staring at her, and what he was thinking.

Suddenly he flung the blanket off his legs, then turned sideways to lay it across the floor on the back wall. 'You're cold. Get on the blanket,' he commanded, oblivious to the chill on his bare legs. 'We'll share it.'

'I'm fine right here,' she started to protest, uncomfortable at the idea of being that close to him.

'Dammit, Marnie, do we have to battle about everything?'

She sighed, shrugged indifferently, then crawled back to the blanket and sat next to him. Once they were settled, backs pressed against the wall, legs stretched out straight toward the fire, he covered them both with a second blanket. He reached across her body to tuck it around her legs, and although the gesture was very businesslike there was something tender and solicitous about it, too.

'There. That's better, isn't it?'

She nodded.

'Good. Then let's eat, drink and be merry,' he said lightly, unpacking food and the Thermos from his own backpack.

She looked at him steadily. 'For tomorrow we may die?'

His jaw tightened, but that was the only indication that he had even heard her finish the old quote. 'Here. Drink as much of this as you can.' He passed her the Thermos lid, filled with coffee that was surprisingly still lukewarm. 'We've both started to dehydrate already, so let's down this, then use it to melt some snow. We're going to need a lot of liquid to get down the rest of this mountain.'

Marnie sipped obediently from the cup while he stabbed the top of a can of beans with his pocketknife, then crawled out from under the blanket to set it near the fire. When he came back, she flipped the blanket over his legs with a brisk, impersonal gesture.

His smile was bemused. 'I'm touched that the sight of my naked body moves you so,' he said drily.

She looked up with faint surprise. 'You're not completely naked,' she pointed out, 'but even if you were, I see a lot of that in my work. I guess I'm used to it, just as you are. Do you think of the models you photograph as naked women?'

He thought about it for a moment, then shook his head.

'Well, this is just the same. To me, you look just like another swimming-suit ad.'

His lips pursed and he shook his head a little sadly.

'That's a pretty sad comment on our business, isn't it? We've all become immune to the sight of the human body—the one thing we're supposed to find inspiring. Sometimes I wonder how the models can stand it.'

Marnie looked at him sharply, remembering her own thoughts about that very thing earlier in the day, thinking how odd it was that this man of all men would make the same observation. 'Yes,' she replied quietly, 'I guess it is.'

He nodded, then refilled her cup from the Thermos.

'How much further do you suppose it is to the bottom?'

'If we're really at the tree-line, we've come almost a third of the way.'

'A third?' Marnie kept her voice casual. 'That's all?'

'That's all.'

She blew a sigh through her cheeks and stared at the fire, thinking of Tiffany. Less than a third of the way, she thought bitterly, after nearly three hours of pure hell. They'd never make it in time. In time? Who was she kidding? They'd never make it, period. Neither one of them could hold up through another six hours like the last three. A brilliantly clarified memory of what it had been like stabbed through her mind, then sank to her stomach in an icy lump of terror. She dealt with it the way she dealt with all other destructive emotions—she ignored it. 'We'll never make it, you know,' she said expressionlessly.

Ross was silent for so long that she almost forgot he was there. It was unnerving, hearing her announce impending doom with all the emotion of a newscaster reading off stock prices. He was beginning to wish he *had* made this trip with a normal, terrified woman. Even a hysteric would be preferable to someone who had no emotions at all. 'Here.' He handed her a packet of dried fruit and nuts.

'I'm not really hungry.'

He pushed the packet firmly into her hand. 'Nevertheless, you'll eat.'

He was right about that much. After that first, desultory nibble, her body's instincts took over, and she couldn't seem to stop. The mindless survival instinct demanded more and more fuel for the furnace of her body, and without thinking about it she obeyed. Fifteen minutes later she sagged back against the wall and shook her head at the astonishing evidence of what they had eaten scattered around them. There were an even dozen empty trail-mix packets, several candy-bar wrappers, and an empty bean can.

'I suppose we'd better get started,' she said.

Ross looked at her with disbelief. 'Do you really love mountain climbing that much, or are you just plain suicidal?'

She looked away and pursed her lips. 'I just want to get it over with.'

'It'll be over with a whole lot faster than you think if I go out there in wet clothes.' He crawled out from under the blanket and over toward the fire to feel the trousers and legwarmers stretched out on the floor. He turned the clothes over, leaned out to place another branch on the fire, then dropped back on his haunches and looked at Marnie expectantly. 'Warm enough?'

'It was warmer with another body under this blanket,' she confessed, then looked down quickly when she realised how that had sounded.

Ross chuckled as he made his way back to her. 'Don't worry, Marnie. I'm not reading innuendo into anything tonight. Body heat is body heat in conditions like this. Besides, the thought of making sexual advances in the middle of a blizzard death march is a little too wild even for me.'

She wondered if he would have felt that way if Tiffany or Bett had been here instead of her. The thought irritated her, and she inched slightly away from leg contact under the blanket.

'Stop pretending to be such a prude,' he yawned, pressing his leg insistently against hers. 'This is survival, not a pass.'

'I'm not pretending!' she said without thinking, clamping her mouth closed just a little too late.

He feigned shock. 'You mean, you really *are* a prude?' She glared at him until he laughed. 'I thought you were used to naked men. You see a lot of them, remember?'

She crossed her arms angrily at his sarcasm and scowled into the fire. 'I *see* them, I don't have them pressed up against me.'

He turned his head very slowly to grin at her. 'Not ever?' he asked playfully.

'Oh, shut up,' she grumbled, but there was no malice in her tone.

'We can't shut up,' he said mildly. 'We'd fall asleep in no time, and that, I'm afraid, is against the rules. Rest, but no sleeping allowed. So pick a subject. We'll have a deep, meaningful conversation.'

He'd taken one of her hands in his, and was turning it over in his palm, examining it with a bemused smile. 'Such a capable hand,' he said. Marnie snatched it away, embarrassed, and tucked it under the blanket.

'Not quite what you're used to photographing, is it?' she grumbled.

'God, no,' he chuckled, remembering an endless series of narrow, bejewelled fingers with long, enamelled tips, dangling at the ends of countless women's arms—alien, unnatural appendages with no imaginable function. 'More like what I dream of photographing.'

She jerked her head to look at him, suspecting sarcasm, and he laughed at her expression.

'Is that so hard to believe? That Ross Arnett would like to photograph real people for a change?'

She almost answered with an immediate affirmative, and then she remembered the picture of Cari Blake; the *real* Cari Blake, the woman all the other photographers had missed. 'You're in a strange business for a man who wants to photograph real people,' she said instead.

He expelled a long sigh of disappointment. 'I am, indeed. It's not exactly what I had in mind when I first picked up a camera.'

'And what did you have in mind?'

He shrugged disparagingly. 'Grandiose, juvenile ideas about moving people with my work; capturing that single glance, that one unguarded moment when the eyes tell the real story about a real person—that's what most photographers are, you know: frustrated storytellers.' He paused and sighed. 'Unfortunately the world doesn't like looking at real life very much. The glitz we deliver pays much more.'

Marnie's brow twitched at the unexpected disdain in his voice. 'Maybe you're underestimating your audience. Did you ever offer them anything else?'

'You mean *serious* photography?' His voice crackled with sarcasm. 'Photos that actually said something? What for?'

'How about for your own self-respect?' she asked a little too sharply. 'It's obvious that you hate what you're doing, and you don't think very much of the people you work with.'

'Speak for yourself, Marnie.'

She looked down and fumbled with the blanket, disturbed by his perception.

He watched her silently, wondering what was going on behind those large, dark eyes, and why knowing was suddenly so important. 'How about you?' he asked her. 'You're not any happier with your job than I am with mine. What would you really like to do?'

She laughed a little, and without thinking, said, 'Nothing. Absolutely nothing. It's the one thing I've never had time for.'

'Marriage? Children?' He hesitated.

She squirmed under the blanket and frowned.

'No?' he prompted.

'I didn't say that.'

'You didn't have to. I could see it in your face.'

'A lot of women choose not to marry and raise families these days,' she said defensively. 'There's nothing wrong with that. I just don't have time for it.'

He was watching her face so intently that it made her nervous. 'You're afraid of it——'

'Certainly not. I just don't choose it, that's all.'

He went on as if she'd said nothing. 'And that's why you fight anyone who tries to get too close.'

'I don't do that!' she almost shouted, glaring at him.

He tipped his head slightly and smiled. 'Isn't that what you've been doing with me?' he asked gently.

'No!' she snapped, trying to turn away, but his hand caught her chin and held it as he stared into her eyes.

'You've been finding reasons to fight with me ever since the moment we met, Marnie; and I'm just beginning to realise that it wasn't because you *didn't* like me, it was because you did. Maybe so much so that it scared you.'

She held her breath like a wilful child while her eyes flashed indignation. 'That's ridiculous!'

He shook his head with a sad smile. 'I don't think so, Marnie. I think you felt the attraction every bit as much as I did.' Her breath caught in her throat as she stared at him, trying to read his eyes. Every bit as much as he did? He saw the suspicion in her glance and smiled. 'The only difference is that you're fighting it. You're afraid to love, aren't you? Afraid of the responsibility.' He moved one finger from her chin to brush lightly across her lips. She wanted to jerk away from his touch, but somehow she couldn't. His eyes held her. 'Love doesn't have to be a burden, Marnie,' he whispered. 'It isn't supposed to be one person always taking care of another. Sometimes, when it's good, two people come together to share, and there are no strings attached, no conditions.'

It was a line. It had to be. And, God help her, she wanted to believe it so badly that it was working. 'You're seducing me,' she murmured in surprise, and for some reason that made him laugh.

'I suppose I am.' He put out one arm and drew her close against his side, but it was like embracing a stone column.

'Why?'

'Why?' He pulled away slightly to stare at her in disbelief, then sighed, exasperated by the question. 'If you have to ask that question, I don't think I know how to answer it.' His hand moved on her shoulder.

'It's a physical thing,' she muttered. 'That's all.'

'Of *course* it's a physical thing! Everything is! We're happy, we smile; we're sad, we cry. That's how people express emotions, you know. Physically.' Then he paused, frowning at her. 'Except for you, of course,' he said bitterly. 'Unlike the rest of us poor mortals, you can control all your emotions, just as you control everything else.' He shook his head and grimaced angrily. 'Well, good for you. They can put that on your tombstone. "Here lies Marnie Weston. She never lost control." ' But then he felt her stiffen and turned to look at her face, already a bright, furious red, and realised that she might be able to control every other emotion with him, but not her temper.

He amended the imaginary inscription with a slow smile. 'Correction—"She never lost control—except with Ross Arnett. He made her madder than hell." ' His smile warmed slightly. 'And that, Marnie, may be the single greatest achievement of my life.'

She glared at him, but the corner of her mouth twitched slightly. 'You're an impossible man.'

'But irresistible,' he teased, pulling her closer.

'To other women, maybe, not to me!'

'Especially to you.'

She stiffened even more, then, out of sheer tiredness, leaned into the circle of his arm. It was like the abrupt toppling of a felled tree, the way she tilted toward him, but it was a beginning.

'There,' he murmured, rubbing his chin against her hair. 'That's better. Lean on someone else for a change.'

'Oh, honestly!' She jerked away and sat forward, hugging her elbows in the age-old body language of self-imposed isolation. 'I don't need anyone to lean on.'

He snapped her back into his embrace with one clean pull, then locked his arm around her shoulder, pinning her to his side. More maddening than the restraint was his low chuckle. 'That's what makes it so good,' he said over her impotent squirming. 'We don't need each other for anything, but the attraction is still there.'

She quieted suddenly, and the sounds of the storm outside intruded once again. She listened to the howl of the wind, like a wild animal kept at bay by the fire, and felt the slow, circular caress of his hand on her shoulder.

'Are you warm enough?' he murmured solicitously, and she flashed back to her mother leaning over her bed, asking that same question whenever she'd been sick in bed as a child. For the first time in years, she relived the feeling of being safe and warm and cared for, and the feeling was heartbreakingly good.

'Yes,' she whispered, letting tense muscles relax, thinking that it might not hurt to lean on this man, just for a moment. 'I'm warm enough.'

She was warmer, in fact, than she had ever been in her whole life. She blinked slowly at the fire, understanding that Ross was doing what all the tabloids said he did best—manipulating women—and, objectively, she had to appreciate his skill. He was Ross Arnett, after all, stuck in a mountain cave in the middle of a blizzard with a woman, and seducing that woman had to be as natural for him as breathing was for other men. It should have made her even more resentful, more invincible than ever to whatever attraction she felt for him; but he had seduced her with the truth, and it was that she was responding to.

He was right, after all. She *had* pulled away from any relationship that threatened to become close, partly because she remembered the awful responsibility of love, and partly because she remembered the agonising emptiness when that responsibility ended. She could never risk giving that much of herself again, and the patience she had learned with Jimmy had served her well. It had been so easy to lock away the traitorous emotions that made you vulnerable, to appear cool, collected, so much in control that other people always kept their distance, a little put off by such reserve. It had been lonely, but it had been safe.

Until now. Until this man came along, drawing

emotions from her like water from a well, shattering that carefully cultivated image of control without any effort at all. She wondered if he had any idea how powerful he really was; and then she wondered if what he had said was true—that it was possible to experience love without the terror of that responsibility, with no strings attached, no conditions . . . what would it be like to be free to experience such a thing, even for a moment?

She noticed now that he had been strangely quiet, that somehow her hand had found its way into his under the blanket, and that his thumb was rubbing up and down the side of her forefinger, making the skin there tingle.

She shifted against him slightly, and inadvertently pressed the soft swell of her breast against his side. He pulled in a sharp breath and held it.

Her eyes widened and her lips parted at the intensity of his reaction. It was a response she had never inspired in a man before, and the power it implied was strangely thrilling. With almost clinical detachment, she wondered if she could repeat it, and moved against him again.

'Mar-nie,' he whispered through his teeth, his eyes closed, the pressure of his hand around hers increasing until it was almost painful. 'You're the one with all the control, remember. Not me.'

She felt the brush of his breath against her forehead, stirring the dark tendrils of hair against skin, and wondered if her eyes were as big as they felt. The hand he still held felt hot, and she imagined she could feel the roughness of his leg through her slacks. So

many tactile sensations crowded nerves she never
knew she had, sending scrambled, frantic impulses to
muscles that didn't know how to respond, except to
press her more firmly against him, but that was more
than enough.

He jerked away from the stone wall and twisted his
upper body to face her, grabbing her arms with such
suddenness that her head fell back on her shoulders.
And then, instead of pulling her close, which she
expected, he just held her there, staring into her
startled eyes, his brows lowered, the muscles of his
jaw held painfully rigid.

There was something about the force of the act, the
pressure of his fingers against her arms, the barely
restrained power she saw in his eyes, that made her
lips part and the breath catch in her throat. She
thought she might still be able to stop it, perhaps with
a cold glance, or a slight pull backward—control was
still within her grasp—but then she heard the sound of
his breathing even over the wail of the wind outside,
and control didn't seem so important any more.

'Marnie,' he murmured, his eyes narrowing beneath
the lowered black of his brows, and the word was a
warning.

She answered by closing her eyes, and in the
blackness she felt herself being drawn slowly forward
by arms that quivered from the effort of restraint; and
then she felt lips, surprisingly hot lips, nipping at the
corners of her mouth, brushing against the skin of her
cheeks, becoming as frantic in their motion as the
breathing that was his and hers echoing in her ears.

She felt the painful restraint of clothing over

breasts that had suddenly become swollen, and when they finally met the wall of his chest she opened her mouth to cry out, only to have it covered with his as he grabbed the back of her neck and pulled her fiercely into the kiss. Then somehow she was on her back and he was bent over her, his eyes dark with intent as they searched hers, his mouth open, drawing in breaths so rapid that they almost frightened her. She felt the trembling of his hand through her sweater as it moved from the pulse at her throat to the throb of her breast, and when her back arched involuntarily at his touch his hand moved frantically under her sweater, released the front clasp of her bra, and cradled a bare breast in a rough, exquisitely hot palm.

There was a near-madness in his eyes that glittered most sharply when her body responded to his touch, as if the challenge had not been simply to possess her, but to make her want to be possessed. Even knowing this, Marnie was helpless to control her own hands or breathing, or the sweet, undulating ache that rolled again and again through her body.

In thoughts so distant she could barely discern them, she wondered if that was all she was to Ross—merely the challenge of seeing a supremely controlled woman totally out of control under his touch. But then his fingers grazed her belly and slid downward, and, although physically he commanded her completely, her mind soared, free at last.

CHAPTER TEN

MARNIE'S hand lay lightly curled on Ross's chest, just a few inches from her face. For perhaps the tenth time in the last thirty minutes, she rotated her wrist carefully and squinted at the face of her watch, then sighed as she glanced over at the fire. By now it had consumed its last branch, and only a scant nest of glowing embers remained. It was time.

A single blanket had not been much protection from the uneven stone floor. The chill had long since penetrated to stiffen her muscles, and the hip she had bruised in the restaurant throbbed in complaint. Still, she would never again be quite as reluctant to leave a bed.

She postponed it for just one moment more, thrilling to the deep, regular thud of Ross's heart beneath her ear, savouring the warm hammock of his arm under her shoulders, wondering if she would ever hear and feel such things again.

He barely stirred as she slipped out from under the blanket and dressed hurriedly in the faint, cool light of the lantern. When she was finished, she knelt at his side, hands splayed wide on her thighs, and gazed down at him, content for the moment to simply see his face.

He looked like an idealistic charcoal sketch of a

man, still a study of light and darkness. Only the intense blue of his eyes ever broke the pattern of black against white, and his eyes were closed now. His lashes cast a shadow of tiny lines across his cheek that looked like they had been drawn there with a finely tipped pen. Even in sleep, there was nothing soft about his features. They were sharply etched on the background of his face, as if strength and will were meant to be clearly visible. He was breathtakingly beautiful, and as she looked at him she felt a powerful, primitive surge of possession that made her blush, as if she had spoken her feelings aloud.

It hadn t been the way she had imagined her first experience with love would be, although it had been precisely what he had promised. No murmured endearments, no frantic words of love, none of the responsibility those words would imply. Her lips twitched ruefully. No strings attached, Marnie. No conditions. Just the way you like your relationships, right?

But it wasn't right. Not any more. Jimmy had taught her the high price of love's commitment, and she'd shied away from it ever since, throwing up a shield of coldness that no one could penetrate. But then Ross Arnett had cracked that shield, reached inside, and somehow it didn't seem to matter that anger was the first emotion he'd pulled out; all the others had trailed obediently behind, like beads on the same necklace. She greeted them one by one, like old friends she hadn't seen in a long time. Fear, guilt, loneliness, grief—such painful emotions that she had vowed to keep them buried for ever; and yet they were part of the human spirit, and without them she had been somehow incomplete, unable to relate to anyone. Without them, she had been just as dead as Jimmy was.

It occurred to her for the first time that perhaps facing emotions required more strength than keeping them hidden, and the thought made her smile sadly. All these years she'd thought everyone else had been weak, letting love and hate and rage and sorrow advertise their humanity; and all the time they had been the strong ones. She'd been patient, unflappable Marnie, the great peacemaker, incapable of anger . . . and equally incapable of the love that was the flip side of the same coin. How bitterly ironic that the man who had shown her all this had done it under her own terms, terms that now seemed stupid and meaningless—no commitments, no conditions. It wasn't what she had wanted after all, but it was all he had offered, and all she had any right to expect.

She stared down at Ross's face, mourning the loss of what she had disdained for so long, what she wanted now more than anything, forgetting to control the tears that were gathering in the corners of her eyes.

Without realising it, she began to rock back and forth in the universal motion of grief for something lost for ever, and it was this sorrowing woman that Ross saw first when he opened his eyes.

His hand shot from beneath the blanket to enclose her wrist, and Marnie jumped, her eyes jerking to his. Her lips quivered in a tremulous smile, and she asked the only question that had any importance, hoping against hope that he would give the last half-hour of her life meaning with his response. 'No strings attached?' Her voice trembled. 'No conditions?'

His chin lifted slightly, as if recoiling from a blow, then his eyes steadied and focused on hers. 'No strings attached,' he said tonelessly.

Her head bobbed once in a jerky nod, then she closed her eyes and sighed.

She didn't know how long she sat there on her knees with her eyes closed, but when she finally opened them again, Ross was fully dressed, sitting opposite her, dark brows lowered in a frown that was inexplicably furious. She puzzled a little over his anger, then noticed the tight lines of frustration around his mouth.

'We have to leave, Marnie. We've waited too long as it is.'

Ah. So that was it. The little liaison had taken too much time.

'I know,' she said in a small voice. Her throat constricted with the sudden understanding that what had happened within this shelter would not survive the short trip to the entry. Once they passed through that portal, this world would evaporate, and the real world would intrude. Only six feet separated what had been from what would be, and suddenly she couldn't bear to think of crossing that distance.

She had surrendered so much more than her body this night, and as she looked into his eyes she wondered if perhaps she shouldn't tell him that. The prospect made her shudder as she imagined his response. He had promised her closeness without conditions, and by her acquiescence she had agreed to those terms. Would he be angry, or only amused to learn that the woman who avoided commitments had changed her mind, and now wanted commitment from him? He would laugh, she decided finally, to hear how very much importance she had placed on what happened between them, and she didn't think she could bear that. He was a man of the world, after all, accustomed to one-night affairs and the sophistication of women who knew when to let go.

It suddenly occurred to her that she could be one of those women, or at least pretend to be. She'd always been very good at pretending.

She composed her features immediately into the old, familiar mask of placidity she had worn for years. 'It'll take me just a minute,' she said coolly.

She couldn't quite read his expression, but as it turned out she didn't have to. He turned quickly and moved away in the unmistakable body language of rejection. She stayed still for a moment, devastated, her eyes on his back as he hurriedly bundled their remaining supplies into the backpacks.

She concentrated on zipping up her snowmobile suit as if it were the world's most challenging mechanical problem. Then she directed her attention to the blankets, folding them into meticulous rectangles that would fit in the packs, trying not to think of what had happened between those rough layers of wool. God, this was hard. Why didn't he say something?

'I'm ready,' she said finally. Her voice cracked.

He looked over his shoulder in her general direction, but avoided her eyes. 'Good. Eat another one of these before we leave.' He tossed her a candy-bar that landed close to her knees.

Her stomach knotted as she reached for it. He had thrown it so offhandedly, like a scrap to a dog. She was so stricken by the impersonal gesture that she forgot to guard her expression.

'Marnie? What is it?'

She glanced up quickly.

Their eyes met and locked, his strangely intent, as if he were waiting for something; hers veiled.

'What were you thinking just then?' he asked, so softly she could barely hear him over the wind outside. The wind. My God, she had actually forgotten the storm. They had locked that out along with everything else, but now it, too, crept back into being.

She licked her lips nervously. There was a terrible, agonising temptation to tell him the truth, his amusement be damned, but the impulse passed quickly. 'Nothing, really. I was just worrying about Tiffany.'

His brow cleared, but his eyes darkened. 'Tiffany,' he repeated tonelessly. 'I see. Well, we're all worried about Tiffany. That's what we're doing here, remember?'

His voice sounded so harsh, so unlike . . . She shook her head to banish the memory and tried to sound casual. She failed miserably. Her words came out brittle instead. 'Speaking of that, there's one thing no one thought to ask you up in the restaurant; maybe because no one wanted to hear that there was no good answer.'

He lifted one brow questioningly.

'Assuming that we do manage to get down this mountain alive, how are we going to get the insulin back up?'

It was what this trip was all about, the one thing that should have been uppermost in his mind, and yet his mouth tightened in distaste, as if he didn't want to talk about it. 'I'll manage,' he said gruffly, shrugging into his jacket.

First person singular, Marnie thought miserably, but the misery didn't emerge in her question, only scepticism. 'How?'

'Trust me. I've got it all worked out.'

'I want to know how,' she said stubbornly, fighting the traitorous quivering of her lips by forcing them into a determined pout. Dammit, he was discarding her completely, like a disposable article that had served its purpose and could now be cast aside. 'I have a stake in this, too, you know,' she blurted out. 'I'd like to know that this nightmare hasn't been all for nothing.'

He sucked in his breath and stared at her without saying a word. She cleared her throat and blundered on.

'I've considered all the reasonable options.' She ticked them off on her fingers, avoiding his eyes. 'No chopper could land on the peak in these winds, so that's out. Hiking back up would take too long, and not even a snowmobile could negotiate the trail, so what does that leave?' She looked at him defiantly.

'The obvious.'

Her laugh was pathetically weak, breathy. 'And what, pray tell, is the obvious?'

His lips lifted, but the smile never touched the blue chips of his eyes. Her heart skipped a beat when his shoulders lifted in a shrug. 'The fastest way up, and the fastest way down. The gondola, of course.'

'The gondola,' she repeated stupidly, her thoughts scrambling for an insight into how on earth he thought he could move the gondola without electricity. She never asked the question. His response had been too certain, somehow irrefutable. Besides, from the look in his eyes at that moment, it seemed almost reasonable that he would have the power to turn the mighty gears through the force of his will alone.

She satisfied herself by mumbling, 'I'll believe it when I see it.'

His look was more frigid than anything that waited for her outside. 'I don't know why you would. You haven't believed anything you've seen so far.'

She jerked her head quickly to look at him, a last shining vestige of hope glimmering in her eyes, but he had already bent to wrap the blankets around his thighs. She watched the procedure mindlessly as the glimmer of hope gradually faded, and finally went out.

A few moments later she was stooped at the small opening to the cave, her mittened hands braced on the rock walls to either side. She stared out at the impossibly heavy snowfall. She had forgotten how bad the conditions had been, and by now they had grown worse. Even on this side of the mountain face the wind had grown savage, and she doubted seriously that either of them could remain upright against its gusts for long. But that wasn't what made her hesitate to follow Ross outside. It was what she was leaving behind that held her there, immobile.

Nothing, she reminded herself. Nothing is what you're leaving behind, and Tiffany's life depends on taking just this one little step. Just the first one will be hard. The rest, no matter how violent the storm, will be much, much easier.

And, with that thought bolstering her, she stepped from the shelter to the outside, from dream to reality, from hope to despair.

She only faltered once, at the first switchback, when something she couldn't control made her pause long enough to look backward. It was a futile gesture. The driving snow obliterated their tracks almost as soon as their feet lifted from them. Seeing anything beyond that, back as far as the cave where she had found love and lost it, was simply impossible. It was as if it had never existed at all.

'What's wrong?' Ross shouted over the scream of the wind. 'Why did you stop?'

She brushed furiously at the eye openings in her mask, shook her head, and motioned him to go on. For some reason he remained still, staring at her through the slit in his face coverings while the storm raged around them. Then, preposterously, he pulled off one mitten, drew the camera from beneath the layers of wool, and snapped her picture. The light of the flash exploded again and again in Marnie's mind as she slammed her eyes closed, and she cursed him silently, bitterly, for recording the moment of her despair.

Again they slid down rock steps on their seats, then trudged down the slope, around the mountain's spine, and into the worst of the wind. They bent forward, heads down and turned, shoulders hunched, and plodded mindlessly forward like two machines whose ultimate purpose had been forgotten. Once again their bodies became numb with cold, their eyes watered and their feet stumbled; and once again the challenge was not to get down the mountain, the challenge was simply to take the next step.

On a clear summer day, Mount Hazard hikers delighted in the novelty of walking next to the very tops of towering pines whose trunks stabbed into the mountainside far below. Gradually, as the trail sloped downward, the walkers would leave the fragile tips overhead to pace next to the uppermost branches, and then the mighty trunks themselves. Because the wind-driven snow blocked them from view, Marnie and Ross didn't notice the trees until the effects of their protection became obvious. As the trunks thickened around them, the wind became less forceful, the snow less driven, and the air less cold. By the time they reached the bottom of the fourth set of rock steps, the conditions had improved tenfold.

'Damn! It's almost tropical down here, isn't it?' Ross shouted elatedly, pulling out the camera and snapping yet another shot of Marnie.

At first the very idea of the photographs had infuriated her, and she did her best to frustrate his efforts, dodging to one side, turning her head whenever he'd turned around, camera in hand. How mad it had seemed to be struggling simply to survive, breathless and exhausted, while Ross blithely snapped photograph after photograph as if they were on some harmless outing. It went beyond eccentricity, all the way to obsession, and she hated him for it. But she was tired of wasting what little extra strength she had dodging the blinding flash. It just didn't seem to matter any more.

There was certainly no monetary value to the humiliating shots of her blundering awkwardly down the face of this damn mountain, but when she thought about it she could well imagine them in Ross Arnett's private album, brought out for the amusement of friends. 'And this is that make-up person, Marnie something-or-other. Did I tell you about her? Chased me down the side of Mount Hazard in a blizzard, she was so eager.'

She saw and heard nothing but the imagined scenario in her mind, and her face burned with shame behind her mask.

'Hold it!' A hand grabbed her viciously from behind and spun her around. 'Where do you think you're going?'

She'd been stomping along so furiously that she had passed him without realising it, and was now tugging him along by the tightened rope that bound them together.

'We're stopping here,' he said sternly. 'It's time to rest.'

Rest? Her lips parted in dismay. What would they do if they stopped to rest? Huddle side by side and talk companionably about the state of world politics?

'No,' she panted. 'Not yet. I'm not tired yet.'

She saw the wary frown between the slit in the scarves, but he merely shrugged, then moved off, once again in the lead.

The trek became progressively easier, so gradually at first that Marnie wasn't aware of it. Eventually, however, her numbed mind took note of the thickening trees, the improved visibility, the reduced amount of snow on the ground. The wind still howled noisily far overhead, but its fury failed to dip into the shelter of the pine trunks that grew more numerous with every step they took. It was no longer necessary to lift her knees to waist level to clear the drifts, and the fallen snow that barely cleared her boot-tops was soft and fluffy, easy to push through. She didn't realise how quiet it had become until Ross spoke.

'That's far enough, Marnie,' he said in a normal voice. 'We have to rest now.'

'No.' She tried to push past him, but he grabbed her arms and jerked her to a halt.

He held her for a moment, his eyes watchful, as if he expected she would bolt and make a run for it. Finally he dropped his hands and nodded toward the enormous base of a nearby tree. They sagged to its base together, both breathing hard from exertion.

Marnie stared straight ahead, painfully conscious of his arm pressed against hers, his chest rising and falling rapidly at the very edge of her peripheral vision. Being this close, and this far apart, was suddenly unbearable. She tugged angrily at the rope that tied them together. 'Is this really necessary any more?'

He looked around as if he hadn't noticed the

improved visibility until this moment. Within the shelter of the trees, it was no longer a blizzard, just a steady, heavy snowfall. It was unlikely that they would become separated now, especially if they used both lights.

'I guess not,' he said quietly, bending to release the complex knot at his waist. 'Here.' He handed her the end of the rope. 'You're a free woman.'

Her vision blurred as she stared down at the frayed yellow cord in her hand, realising it was ridiculous to attach any symbolic significance to the moment, but unable to help herself. It was the very last thing that had connected them. She almost burst into tears. Horror at the prospect of that final humiliation made her jump to her feet and rip the ski mask from her head, as if that would keep the tears from falling. 'I don't need this any more,' she mumbled distractedly to explain her gesture. 'It's too hot.'

The camera flahsed up at her before she realised he'd taken it out.

'Aren't you out of film *yet*?' she snapped, stomping over to a tree that faced his, sliding down until she sat at the base. Only a few feet separated them, and she had to keep her knees bent to avoid entangling their legs. From this distance she could see his eyes clearly. They seemed almost colourless in the fluorescent glow of the camping light.

He ignored her question and just stared at her as he unwound the scarves that covered his face. She almost wished they were back in the freezing wind, the horizontal snow, if only so this moment could have been avoided.

He was no longer an unidentifiable lump of cast-off clothing; the bulky leader she could dissociate from the man in the shelter. The man in the shelter was back again, and looking at his face was the hardest thing she'd ever done in her life.

His hair was flattened against his skull from the pressure of the scarves, a thin black frame surrounding the lighter picture of his face. As he looked at her, he stripped off his mitten and ran his fingers back through it, lifting it away from his head. There was something terribly intimate about the way he stared at her as he performed this rite, something strangely erotic, as if he were commanding her with his eyes to witness an act every bit as personal as undressing. A stray lock fell across one brow in an insolent slash, and it was all Marnie could do to keep from leaping forward to push it aside. Her fingers curled inside her mittens with the effort of keeping still, and an ache of longing tightened her throat.

It wasn't so much to ask, was it? To be able to touch him one last time, just to brush a single lock of hair from his forehead? And then she wouldn't ask for anything more.

Her face remained passive, reflecting none of this longing as she turned it quickly away.

'It's our last stop, Marnie.' He waited, as if he expected her to say something.

She examined her mittens intently. 'Oh? We're that close to the bottom?'

'I think so. We made pretty decent time, considering. You can be proud of yourself, Marnie.'

Her gaze was ice. 'Can I?'

'Of course you can. You were . . .' He hesitated, then shrugged.

'A good sport?' she asked, her tone brittle.

'Marnie . . .'

She cut him off by jumping to her feet. 'We'd better get going.'

He rose slowly, his eyes narrowed in exasperation, his tone sharp. 'All right. We'll go. But there are some things that need to be said between us. We'll get together later, after this is all over.'

Her laugh was high-pitched and slightly false. We'll get together, we'll have lunch, we'll talk soon—the lame phrases danced through her mind in cruel, bright mockery. 'Of course we will, Ross. We'll get together soon—and talk about old times.' Even to her, her voice sounded remarkably like Tiffany's at her cutting, cynical best.

She would have felt the scalding rage in his eyes even if she hadn't seen it.

'You really are a cold bitch, aren't you?' he spat out the words.

She tugged at her mittens and brushed at the front of her suit, then looked up at him with a cool, implacable gaze.

Ross stared at her for a moment, then without another word turned and led the way down the mountain.

CHAPTER ELEVEN

'DEAR-LORD-IN-HEAVEN!' The words tumbled from Buzz's mouth in one breathy, disbelieving exhale.

Ross and Marnie had just clumped into the base station, slamming the door behind them, catching Buzz in mid-stride on the way to his tiny office. When he'd gathered his wits sufficiently to command the muscles of his eyes, they raced up and down the two snowy apparitions as if he expected them to disappear at any moment. 'Dear Lord in Heaven,' he repeated tonelessly, like a child entranced with the sound of his first spoken sentence.

'Hi, Buzz,' Ross said casually. 'Got any coffee? That hiking trail isn't quite the lark you said it was. We're a little tired.'

The old man's mouth worked soundlessly for a moment, then he blinked and seemed to come to life. 'Oh, for crying out loud,' he muttered, exasperated. 'You two fools hiked down that mountain in this weather?' He transformed instantly from a shocked old man to a blustering mother hen, perturbed at the impudence of her chicks. 'You get yourselves out of those wet things and get into my office,' he ordered brusquely. 'I'll be back as soon as I find you some dry clothes.'

Marnie's shoulders slumped as soon as he left, as if

his presence had been all that was holding her erect.

'Here,' Ross said gently, shedding his mittens, reaching under Marnie's chin for the zipper of her suit. 'Let me do that.'

She closed her eyes, too exhausted to protest, wincing slightly at the crisp, cold-air scent of his hands, hating herself for wanting to pull the smell into her lungs and never exhale again. Her thoughts flashed back to childhood, coming into the warm farm kitchen from outside, inhaling the magical, mingled scents of gingerbread and hot cocoa while her mother helped her out of the complex mystery of her snowsuit. She felt all those old feelings again now, as Ross undressed her with poignant tenderness, pulling the mittens from her limp hands, sliding the suit from her arms. He bent to take off her heavy boots as she stood on one leg like a trusting child, her hand braced on his shoulder for balance.

She felt childlike when she finally stood before him in just her rose slacks and sweater. He cupped her chin in one hand and brushed the damp strands of her hair from her forehead with the other, his lips twitching as if he were afraid to speak. 'That's better,' he murmured finally. 'That's my Marnie.'

She raised molten, dark eyes to his blue ones, confused by this sudden tenderness, too tired to care if he knew. 'What do you want from me?' she whispered plaintively, because the moment his hands had touched her she'd decided she had to know.

'Just one more night.' His breath tiptoed across her face, gently delivering the horrible truth. 'That's all I ask. Just one more night.'

She felt the air whistle through her lips in a rush, and wondered if it could possibly feel much worse than this to die. One more night. Her mind twisted in a wry smile long before the expression found its way to her mouth. She'd been stupidly naïve—again—dreaming of a lifetime with a man who measured relationships one night at a time. She thought in that instant that she would never laugh again, and in the next the sound came out of her mouth. A remote part of her mind congratulated herself on the harsh, coldly amused sound of it.

'Sorry. I'm not interested.'

He pulled his head sharply backward, and for a moment she imagined she saw a flash of pain in his eyes. 'Is that a fact?' he said flatly. 'Well, that's a little hard to believe. The woman up in that cave was sure as hell interested.'

'But we're not in that cave any more, are we?' she retorted calmly. 'We're back in the real world again. Things aren't the same down here.'

She couldn't decide if his facial muscles had relaxed or tensed, but, whichever it was, his expression went suddenly, utterly blank.

'Well, get a move on, you two!' Buzz hustled up from behind, a stack of blue denim draped over one arm, a box of bakery doughnuts clutched under the other. He passed them each a pair of overalls and pushed them toward the restrooms. 'Hurry up and get yourselves changed and into the office. I'll crank up the kerosene heater.'

A few moments later they all sat around a scarred wooden table in Buzz's office. The little kerosene heater had warmed the tiny room almost past the point of bearing. Ross and Marnie sat opposite one another, eyes cast down, looking faintly ridiculous in the ill-fitting overalls of two absent workers. Marnie's was far too large, the cuffs rolled back several times and still hanging over her wrists, while the buttons strained into gaps across Ross's chest.

'I still can't believe you did it!' Buzz was saying. 'Damn! All the way down Mount Hazard in the worst weather we've had in years! You two are really something, you know it? Here. Eat some more, both of you.' He pushed the plate of doughnuts between them.

Ross smiled wearily and held up one hand, palm out. 'Stop fussing, Buzz. We're dry, we're warm, and we've had enough to eat. Now we've got work to do.'

Marnie watched the kind old face carefully as Ross explained the situation on top of the mountain in terse, clipped sentences. Watching Buzz was like reading a book, his expressions reflected his thoughts so clearly. First horror, then dismay, then the ultimate frustration of a man who has finally, reluctantly acknowledged impotence.

'So we've got to get that gondola running,' Ross finished.

Buzz slid to the edge of his well-worn chair, his lips pressed together in a grim line. 'As I told you over the radio, son, that gondola doesn't run without electricity, and that's a commodity we're mighty short of just now.' He gestured toward the kerosene lamps scattered around the room. 'Now I'll call Ski Rescue. Those boys know this old mountain like their own back yards, and once they get here . . .'

'We don't have that kind of time, Buzz,' Ross said quietly. 'We have to get the insulin up there by noon.'

'By noon? Hell, boy, the rescue squad can't even get *here* by noon the way the roads are. Most of them are blown shut already.'

'You've got a SnoCat parked just outside, Buzz. Does it run?'

Marnie cocked her head, vaguely remembering the huge yellow vehicle they'd passed on their way in the door. It had been layered with snow, its half-track treads nearly buried in drifts.

'Does it run?' Buzz echoed, perplexed. 'Of course it runs, but it doesn't run up the side of mountains, and . . .'

'It won't have to go that far,' Ross interrupted. 'Just close enough to the building to connect it to the gondola motor.' He leaned over the table toward the older man, his eyes fiercely alight. 'They run the gondola on Mount Mansard with a gasoline engine. Why not this one?'

Buzz's jaw dropped in slow motion as the idea settled in his mind. 'Use the SnoCat engine to run the gondola?' he murmured, shaggy white brows twitching with the sudden scramble of thought. 'It won't work,' he mumbled, thinking out loud. 'Rpms are different, for one thing . . .'

'It *will* work,' Ross said firmly. 'We can increase the SnoCat's rpms just by stepping on the gas, and we can connect the two motors with gear belts, like this.' He pulled a battered notepad and a pencil stub from the front pocket of Buzz's overalls and began scrawling a baffling series of circles and lines on the crinkled paper. 'Like that, Buzz,' he said, passing the pad across the table. 'Strip two of the belts from the gondola motor and run them right out that big side-window to the SnoCat's main drive. We used to do it on the farm all the time. We'd hook the tractor engine up to the electric hay loader, because we didn't have power in the barn.'

Marnie turned her head slowly to look at him. 'You used to live on a farm?' she asked quietly.

He stared at her for a moment before answering. 'I still do, whenever I get a break in my work.' He smiled pointedly. 'In a dusty, dried-out weatherbeaten town in South Dakota. Not very pretty, and not very fashionable, but everyone who lives there is real.'

Marnie winced at the implication that somehow she wasn't, then pretended indifference and turned away.

'Dammit, boy, this just might work!' Buzz jumped up from the table, the notepad clutched in one hand.

Ross looked up and smiled tiredly. 'It will. The radio went dead before I could tell you to give it a try.'

'Wouldn't have done a bit of good. Bill's the mechanic here, and he left for home the minute the power went. Hope you're as good with a wrench as you are with a pencil, young man. I wouldn't know the first thing about how to make this work.' He was already shrugging into a fur-lined parka, snatching a set of keys from his desk. 'I'll move the 'Cat closer to the building and get that window open. Think you can handle the rest?'

'I can.'

Marnie didn't move as Buzz hustled out of the

office. She just sat there, staring at Ross. 'Can you really make it work?'

Ross blinked once, then let his eyes rest on hers. 'They're just machines, Marnie. Machines are easy.'

Her lower lip quivered and she dropped her eyes to watch her hand toy with the pencil stub he had tossed aside. 'And once it's running, then what?'

'Then we'll bring the gondola down, and I'll ride it back up.'

Marnie's gaze wavered. She almost looked up at him, but she caught herself just in time. 'There's still a storm out there,' she said quietly.

'Should be an interesting ride, don't you think?'

She jerked her eyes upward, trembling when they met his. They stared at each other for so long that they began to look like two subjects of a still-life. Marnie's hand was quiet at last, the forgotten pencil curled inside her fist. Ross moved his own hand very slowly to cover it, but Marnie didn't even glance down. She couldn't take her eyes from his face, and all she could think of was how tired he looked; too tired to take a risky ride up the side of a mountain in a fragile box buffeted by gale-force winds.

'It's too dangerous,' she finally whispered, barely moving her lips.

He was over on her side of the table before her mind had registered his first motion, lifting her by the shoulders, his eyes burning into hers as his fingers pressed deep into her flesh. 'You're not as cold-blooded as you'd like me to believe, are you, Marnie?' he hissed fiercely. 'And you and I aren't finished yet. I don't know why you're pretending we are, and frankly, I don't much care any more.' His mouth crashed down with a ferocity that left her breathless, quivering in his embrace, stunned by the force of her own reaction.

He pulled back finally, releasing her shouders, moving one hand to grasp her firmly at the back of her neck. Her lips remained parted, glistening with the moisture from his kiss. 'It isn't Jimmy this time, is it?' he demanded savagely. 'This time it's just me. Ross Arnett. *I'm* the one you're worried about.'

She swallowed once and tried to catch her breath, tried to ignore the bruising stimulus of her breasts flattened against his chest. 'So?' she breathed weakly. 'So what's wrong with that? I've gotten to know you. Of course I'm concerned. We're . . . friends, in a way.'

'Friends?' he barked a laugh. 'Is *that* what we are?' He caught her head in both hands, tipped it a little to one side, and leaned toward her, his words scraping harshly against the sides of his throat when he spoke. 'Well, then, if friends are what we are, by all means, let's hear it for friendship.'

Not for one moment did it occur to her to fight him. When the roar of the SnoCat engine thundered through the building, vibrating the walls as it came to life, she mistook it for the blood pounding in her ears. She could feel his lips on hers, she could smell the faint freshness of his face, and, finally, she could taste the sweet tartness of his tongue as it forced her lips apart. She had no need to see or hear. She was back in the cave again, feeling the exquisite tingle of swollen breasts meeting the rock of his chest; the sharp complaint of a back arched in a forward thrust; the breathtaking pressure of hip melding into hip.

When he released her mouth long enough to murmur her name against her neck, she threw her head backwards and gasped for breath like a person surfacing from black water for the last time. His lips ground into her neck until she felt his teeth against her skin; his hands slipped beneath her sweater, sliding upwards to cup the full breasts, and when his thumbs grazed her nipples, she cried out softly, then jerked away, startled by the sound she had made.

He stood with his legs slightly apart, his chin tucked, the smouldering blue coals of his eyes barely visible behind shuttered lids. The black of his sweater rose and fell rapidly as he struggled to draw breath. 'Pretend what you like, Marnie,' his voice rasped with triumph, 'but don't expect me to believe you don't still want me. Not after this.' His hand shot out for her and she scrambled backward out of his reach, her eyes wild.

'It's not finished between us,' he growled. 'So help me God, Marnie, it's not finished. You're mine. Whenever I want you.'

'Uh—excuse me.'

She jumped at the sound of Buzz's voice behind her, but she didn't turn around. Her cheeks coloured as she wondered how much he had seen and heard, but she kept her eyes fixed on Ross.

'It's all right, Buzz,' Ross said without looking at him. 'Marnie and I will finish our conversation later.'

He brushed intentionally against her as he walked past, stopped and looked down, clearly amused by her wide-eyed watchfulness. 'Coming, Marnie?' he mocked her, his mouth quirked in a cocky smile.

She took orders obediently for the next half-hour, handing tools to Ross as he hunched over the gondola's gear assembly, passing greasy rubber belts out the window to where Buzz hooked them up to the SnoCat. When Ross pronounced the work finished, she backed away, her head shaking doubtfully. The motor looked like a boy's destructive first experience tinkering with his father's lawn-mower. A chain of rubber belting stretched from a series of graduated gears out the window. She couldn't imagine what Buzz had done with them on the outside, but if it looked anything like what Ross had done in here, the results would have to be disastrous.

'All right, Marnie.' Ross looked up from the motor briefly, swiping at his hair with a hand almost as black. 'You're going to have to start the 'Cat while we keep an eye on the connections. Get out there and have Buzz show you how.'

It was strangely exhilarating, sitting up so far above the ground in the grand yellow machine. She felt tall and competent and strangely removed from the tangle of emotions she battled below. It reminded her of simpler times on her father's tractor, those years before Ross Arnett, when the world was blessedly black and white with the clarity of youthful innocence.

From her lofty perch facing the building, she could see through the window to where Ross stood by the motor, making last-minute adjustments with a wrench. Finally he lifted his head and raised one arm. Buzz duplicated the gesture from the front of the

SnoCat, his eyes fixed on the monster's mighty engine. Marnie nodded once, then started the engine.

The cab trembled, rocked violently, then settled into a regular vibration as the SnoCat roared to life.

'More gas!' Buzz shouted over the mechanical thunder in response to a furious gesture from Ross, and she pressed a little harder on the accelerator.

No one had to tell her it was working. From her position, she was the first to notice the cables in the gondola housing jerk, then grind around their oval guide in the movement that would bring the gondola down. Buzz was elated, hopping up and down in the snow like a demented black elf, but through the window she saw Ross standing calmly with his hands on hips, looking out at where she sat, looking in.

'The radio in the gondola still works.' Buzz stepped out of the snow-crusted cab, which was apparently none the worse for its night dangling in the storm. 'You keep it on all the way up, Ross, hear? I've got the 'Cat's idle locked on the right speed, so Marnie can stay on the radio while I keep an eye on things out here. It's going to be a nasty ride in these winds. You've got to tell us if it gets too bad so we can bring you back down. No point in you ending up smashed on the side of that mountain, you know.'

Ross was smiling at him. 'Thanks, Buzz,' he said quietly, clasping the old man's hand briefly, and then to Marnie, 'Did you find the insulin?'

Without looking at him, she passed him the small plastic case she'd found in Tiffany's bag. He watched her downcast eyes as he tucked the case into a zippered pocket.

'You wouldn't know the woman was desperate to seduce me by looking at her, would you, Buzz?'

Marnie gasped and took a quick step backward, her eyes so appallingly wide that they threatened to absorb the rest of her face. If she hadn't heard it with her own ears, she wouldn't have believed any man capable of such callousness. He was flaunting his power, humiliating her publicly, and she didn't doubt for a moment that Buzz was only the first in a long line of the people he would regale with stories of his mountainside conquest. She felt suddenly ill.

Buzz, at least, had the decency to turn aside, a little embarrassed. The moment he did, Ross grabbed Marnie unceremoniously and kissed her with a thoroughness that drove all thoughts of indignant resistance right from her head. Even as her mind screamed a silent rebellion, her lips betrayed her with their response. The frustration at not being able to control her own body was so great that she almost burst into tears.

'Just for luck,' Ross said lightly, releasing her, flipping a jaunty salute as he climbed into the gondola. 'Start her up, Buzz,' he called out merrily. 'I'm in a hurry to get back down here!'

Buzz released a plaintive sigh, remembering the fierce passions of youth, then glanced at Marnie and smiled. 'You're going to have your hands full with that one,' he said kindly.

'It isn't what you think, Buzz. You don't understand,' she said sadly, not really expecting that he would be convinced.

'Of course I understand, missy. I may be old, but I'm not dead. My eyes still work, and my mind still knows what my eyes see.'

And what you don't see, he'll tell you about later, she thought grimly. Her vision blurred suddenly, and she stumbled blindly through the door and inside to the small office that housed the radio. She crumpled on to the straight-backed chair like a boneless puppet and dropped her head into her hands.

She reached deep inside for the rage she wanted desperately to feel, but all she found was a new kind of sick despair. It seemed pointless, now, to try to deny it. She could pretend coldness and feign indifference all she wanted, but he could shatter the façade whenever he wanted simply by touching her, and he knew it. She was no better, no different from any of the other women he had had, and suddenly she felt deeply sorry for every single one of them who had been as defenceless against him as she was.

No doubt he thought he'd found the perfect playmate—a woman every bit as anxious to avoid the complications of involvement as he was—but it hadn't turned out that way. Of the two of them, it was she, the one who had held back, who was really capable of love. No wonder he had offered a relationship without commitment. He wasn't capable of making one. Had he ever mentioned love? Caring? Did he even grant her one of the pathetically empty compliments he doled out indiscriminately to every other woman he met? No. He didn't even give her that small shred of dignity. So what will you say to him, Marnie Weston? What will you say to this truly emotionless man when he comes rapping at your hotel-room door tonight? 'I'll say, "Come in",' she whispered aloud, devastated by the truth.

'Marnie? Are you there?'

She trembled at the sound of his voice crackling through the speaker. It was distorted, choppy with static, but still, it was his voice. 'I'm here, Ross. How bad is it up there?'

'Not so bad . . .'

He was lying. She could hear the clatter of something rattling around the wind-tossed cab. 'Should we bring you back down?'

His chuckle was rich and dark. 'No, Marnie. Be patient. We'll be together soon enough.'

She closed her eyes, humiliated, and said nothing.

After a long silence his voice came through with surprising clarity. 'Poor Marnie,' he said softly, and this was the cruellest blow of all, that he felt sorry for her. 'You don't even understand it, do you? It's all too new.' His last words of comfort fell like the absent pats of a master on his pet's head. 'But don't worry. You'll get used to it.'

No! her thoughts shrieked in violent rebellion. To have her values repeatedly torn down, her will subverted, the mastery of her own body relinquished to a man who had no conception of the destruction he left behind? Dear God, no. She would never get used to that. She could not allow it to happen.

'Hey!' Buzz greeted her with a smile when she walked toward him.

'He made it,' she said quietly.

Buzz chuckled. 'Of course he did.' He nodded at the markings on the cable that indicated the gondola's position. 'He intended to, and so he did. Man that determined usually finds a way to do what he wants.'

Marnie smiled ruefully. 'He radioed back from the gondola that Tiffany's all right. She was weak, but still hanging on. He's going to stay up there with them for a while.'

'Just as well. The winds are supposed to die down this afternoon. Maybe we can bring them all down at once.' He walked a little closer and looked at her intently. 'What are you up to, missy? You're all dressed up for outside again.'

'Oh.' Marnie glanced down at her snowmobile suit. 'I almost forgot to tell you. One of your co-workers hitched a ride out here on the snowplough, in case you needed a hand. The crew offered me a lift into town, and I'd like to go if you can manage without me.'

'Of course we can, missy.' Buzz smiled at her with genuine affection. 'You get yourself back to the inn and get some rest. Soak in a hot tub, eat a decent meal, then sleep the day away. When your friends come down, we'll all drive over in the SnoCat and have a little celebration. What do you say to that?'

There was something so deep and honest behind the old face, something genuine and permanent that reminded her of her father and made her reluctant to leave him. Suddenly she threw her arms around his bulk and hugged hard, whispering into his parka, 'I'm going to miss you, Buzz.'

The old man started in surprise, then closed his arms in a brusque, fatherly hug. 'And I'll miss you,

Marnie. But we won't say goodbye yet. I'll see you later. I promise.'

She pressed her lips so tightly together that they hurt, then flashed a brief smile and dashed away.

The tall, harried man that helped her up into the giant snowplough frowned at her stricken expression. 'You sure you want to go straight to the train station, miss?'

Marnie settled herself in the tall seat and looked straight ahead though the windscreen. 'You said I could catch the morning train to Chicago if I hurried,' she said. 'And that's the only way out of town, right?'

'You bet it is,' he chuckled softly, grinding the gears as the brutish beast lurched forward. 'Nothing else is moving out of here but the trains, and we've only got that one a day. You seem mighty anxious to get away from our weather,' he teased.

Her smile was thin and tired. 'I never did like blizzards much.'

CHAPTER TWELVE

MARNIE strolled down the long, rutted driveway, her jacket open to the light breeze, her boots squishing in the brown slush of rapidly melting snow. She stopped every now and then to listen to the sounds of spring: the trickle of running water, the hard, bright call of Canadian geese returning home, and the melodic trill of a plain brown sparrow, beautiful at last through his song.

She'd grown deeply attached to the hardy sparrows over the past four months. At first she had been awed by their placid resignation to nature's winter fury; now she was jealous of the joyful, carefree abandon with which they greeted spring. Already they had forgotten the hardships of winter, forgiven nature's cruelty. If only her memory could be so short, then perhaps she could share their joy.

Her parents had been openly delighted by her return home, but secretly concerned at the suddenness of her decision to take a sabbatical from her career. She worked periodically at the local beauty shop, transforming the weathered faces of farm wives, enhancing the fresh beauty of young girls preparing for their first dance; but surely there was no challenge in this, no test of the talents she had perfected in that other world? Besides, something about her was different. There was a sadness behind the great dark eyes that never seemed to go away, even when her laughter bubbled at something that had amused her.

So John and Ethel Weston fretted over the pervasive sombreness of their only remaining child, and supported her in the only way they knew how—silently, and without question, and for that Marnie was grateful.

When she phoned her agent shortly after her arrival to cancel upcoming assignments, Marnie had realised for the first time how little anyone in New York actually knew about her, how friendless and isolated she had really been. Few people knew she had family in Wisconsin, and not one of those knew so much as the name of the town where they lived. That had shocked her initially, and then pleased her in a perverse sort of way. At least she could vanish completely from a life-style that now seemed meaningless.

Occasionally she allowed herself to remember her old life, and always she found herself wondering what she had intended to accomplish. She'd run so frantically from Jimmy's death to the anonymity of the city, away from the only things that had ever been important: home, love, and the steady, inevitable continuation of life, repeating itself in one generation after the other. What had career success been worth after all, measured against such things?

The rumble of Mr Smith's old mail truck pulling away startled her out of her reverie, and she lifted her arm in a wave as he drove away. Her eyes brightened as she pulled the flat brown rectangle from the metal box. She'd ordered some special, hypoallergenic make-up for an older woman who had never been able to use cosmetics, and anticipating her delight made her strangely happy. Wouldn't they laugh at me in New York! she thought with amusement. Here I am, all aquiver because a Wisconsin farm wife can finally darken her lashes. It sounded trivial, but somehow it wasn't.

Her eyes clouded slightly as she saw Tiffany's return address on the box. Damn that agent, anyway. She'd told him over and over not to give out her address. Then she noticed the agency mailing label and sighed with relief. Apparently he had taken the package from Tiffany and sent it on himself.

She opened the box slowly, then hesitated, totally confused by the slender dark volume it contained. Why on earth would Tiffany, of all people, send her a book?

Her breath stopped when she saw the embossed gold lettering on the plain brown cover. *Marnie Against the Mountain*, it read.

She sat right down in the wet, mushy snow at the side of the road and braced the book on her knees. Her hand trembled as she opened the book and read what Tiffany had scrawled inside the front cover. 'Go see him,' the cryptic note said. 'Give the poor guy a break.' The Manhattan address of Ross Arnett Studios was printed neatly beneath.

She turned to the book's first page and pulled in a sharp breath to see her own face staring up at her. All the tumultuous memories of that night, all the things she had spent the last four months trying to forget, flooded through her mind with the force of a tidal wave.

She remembered the shot. He'd taken it just after she'd ripped off her ski mask for the first time, down in the shelter of the trees. She remembered the humiliation and the despair she had felt then, but these were feelings she had never seen on her own face before, feelings she had never permitted expression, because admission of their existence was a defeat in itself. Seeing them now on her own image, and feeling no shame at the unmistakable evidence of her own humanity was a quiet revelation. Perhaps it wasn't so bad, being merely human.

Suddenly the woman in the picture wasn't her any more, it was every woman who had ever felt the grinding finality of despair, and Marnie almost wept at the tragedy in the mournful eyes, because the story they told was everyone's story at one time or another. Sorrow was universal. It belonged to everyone.

She turned the pages slowly, one by one, objectively admiring the genius of a man who had seen the faces of the world reflected in one face. Her eyes blurred as she looked at one captionless photo after another, startled by the crystalline image of emotions she saw in each one, reliving them all, rediscovering the pain and the joy of simply permitting herself to feel.

It was her mother who later happened upon the dedication page Marnie had somehow missed.

'Well, child,' she said softly from her chair by the fire, the book propped open in her lap. Marnie walked over to see what had prompted such a strange tone of wonder, and her mother held up the book so she could read the small block letters on the stark emptiness of a front page. 'For love of Marnie', it said.

She stood quietly behind her mother's chair for a very long time, staring far beyond the walled confines of a farmhouse living-room that hadn't changed in twenty years. Finally she took a deep breath, straightened, and walked to the phone in the front hall to book a flight to New York.

It was a little disorientating, to be wrapped in the quiet of the Wisconsin countryside one day, then battling through the noisy flurry of Manhattan's rush-hour the next. But it was invigorating, too; strangely stimulating. Marnie felt as if she had just wakened from a very long sleep.

The city glittered under the noonday sun with the same shameless pretention she remembered. Glamorous women and tailored men bumped shoulders with raucous cabbies and bizarrely dressed street people, but somehow they all belonged, all melded together to form the incredible, vital glitz that was New York. It was bright, it was loud, it was elegant and shabby all at once, and beneath it all was the surging throb of a million heartbeats pumping the life of the city. Until this moment, Marnie hadn't realised how much she had missed it.

She hesitated in front of the Third Avenue highrise and looked up at the towering wall of glass and steel. Ross's studio was up there somewhere, and she was a little surprised at her eagerness to confront him, and, through him, to confront the truths about herself she'd been hiding from all this time.

His book had done that for her—no matter that he had chronicled a photographic history of just another one of his many conquests, then packaged it for profit. What really mattered was that she had seen herself in his photographs—really seen herself—perhaps for the very first time, and she had discovered to her surprise that she liked what she saw. The woman in the pictures had been alternately challenged, triumphant, and defeated; but, because she had been all of those things, the woman had been whole. Alive. Real. She had finally seen herself with all the the frailties and weaknesses that afflicted any other human being, and somehow she was stronger for it. It gave her licence to be angry, impatient, less than perfect; to fall in love with the wrong man and to lose control in the heat of passion; and not to be diminished by those things. At last, it was all right to feel.

Of course, she would probably never be called 'peacemaker' again. Imperfect people sometimes exhibited perfectly awful fits of temper, and a person with a temper wouldn't hold that deified position for long. But maybe her tumble from that lofty perch of unflappable superiority would make her a little less forbidding. Maybe the common ground of uncontrollable emotions would bring her closer to others with the same weakness, and perhaps among their number she would find her first friends. The thought made her smile.

She glanced in passing at her reflection in the glass door of the building, and gave a short, happy nod of approval. She was celebrating today, and she had dressed for it. She wore a shamelessly expensive blue silk dress with a brightly patterned cape that swirled around her legs when she moved. It made her look exactly the way she felt—alive, bursting with the wonder of it, just like the drab brown sparrow who finally achieved beauty in the glory of a spring song.

The hinge on the tenth floor studio door was broken, and the door slammed behind her, its sound echoing in the huge room. She hadn't intended to make such a startling entrance, but, now that she had, it seemed appropriate.

Half a dozen perfect feminine faces lifted simultaneously under the intense lighting of a beach scene backdrop. Startled, a few bikini-clad figures jumped to their feet, shading their eyes against the lights to see the darkened doorway beyond.

'Dammit!' The rich timbre of his voice rippled along Marnie's nerve-endings, and instead of cringing from it she thrilled to its passage. So, she thought, relishing the tingle that made her feel alive, he still has the power.

The voice assumed a dark, tense shape, rising from behind the camera, spinning in anger to face the door. 'Whoever the hell you are, you just ruined . . .' He broke off suddenly when he saw her.

It seemed odd that he should look just the same, after all this time. The eyes still snapped blue smoke, the black hair still whipped across his brow when he moved, and the body still seemed to crackle with the electric force of contained energy. It was rigid now, every muscle held tightly immobile as he stared at her, almost as though he had suspended life entirely until he could process the evidence of his eyes.

The room seemed to hold its breath, anticipating a clash between the two motionless figures whose eyes had locked with an almost audible force.

Suddenly Ross spun away from her and faced the models, becoming a still-life again for a moment in this new position, then exploding in a flurry of gestures and mumbled phrases, apparently dismissing them. He spoke too softly for Marnie to hear, but apparently his praise was lavish. The nearly naked women clustered around him like adoring children, murmuring words of parting, pressing his hands, kissing his cheeks or his lips, a few even crawling into a brief embrace before scurrying away. Not one left without feeling his touch or hearing a few special, whispered words that made their faces shine.

Marnie watched, stone-faced, as he manipulated them all, working his magic. Grudgingly, she admired his skill at coddling the delicate egos, even as she despised him for doing it.

Eventually, Ross stood alone, watching the women file toward the door where Marnie stood in silence. Once there, they seemed to turn as a body to face him, but the suggestion of orderliness dissolved as they called out individual farewells and waved and blew kisses in what Marnie thought was a particularly juvenile, overdone display.

Ross stood with his hands shoved in his trouser pockets, smiling at them all, and, with that special gift of his that twisted at Marnie's heart, seemed to be smiling at each one individually.

'You've all been wonderful, girls,' he said quietly, but his voice carried easily in the suddenly silent room. 'Every last one of you.' Then he raised his hand, almost in benediction. 'I love you all.'

Marnie stood quietly to one side as the women passed in a line out the door, each one more beautiful than the last, trying to keep his last words from echoing and re-echoing inside her head. There had been a moment—

one foolish, desperately naïve moment—when she had hoped that the dedication page of his book might really have meant something. She'd travelled all this way on that one slender thread of hope, and now, in an instant, it had been snatched away. The phrase 'For love of Marnie' meant no more to Ross Arnett than his parting words to the cluster of women who had just left, words he used so often in his work that they fell automatically from his mouth. Empty, meaningless words.

She straightened her shoulders and looked at him. 'Quite a harem,' she said sarcastically.

He turned his back and bent over his camera. 'They were lovely, weren't they?'

'And you love them all. How touching.'

His head lifted slightly as if he were going to turn to look at her, then stopped.

Marnie waited for him to say something, irritated that he could ignore her like this. 'It must be exhausting,' she drawled after a moment of silence, 'loving so many women all at the same time.'

She saw his shoulders lift in a deep breath, then freeze in position.

'It is, in a way,' he said rigidly. 'I don't think I'll miss it at all.'

Marnie hesitated. 'Miss it?'

He seemed to relax, and bent to peer through the camera lens as if he still had subjects posing before it. 'That's right,' he said casually. 'This was the last layout I'd contracted to do. As of right now, the Ross Arnett Manhattan studio is closed. I'm leaving the city tomorrow.'

'What?' she blurted in disbelief. All she could think of was that if she had waited one more day to fly out here, he would have been gone before she'd had the satisfaction of confronting him. 'Leaving? For where?'

His head whipped around almost before she'd finished the question, and she sucked in a startled breath at the black fury distorting his face. The one thing she hadn't expected was *his* anger.

'What right do you have to ask where I'm going?' he demanded, his voice crackling across the empty space between them. 'You never saw fit to tell me where you were for the last four months!'

'And why should I?' she snapped without even wondering at his sudden rage. 'Where I go and what I do is absolutely none of your business!'

His eyes widened slightly, then he turned back to his camera and spoke without looking at her. His voice was passive now, almost indifferent. 'Fine. And by the same token, where I go is none of your business. Now that we've got that settled, what the hell are you doing here?'

Marnie hesitated again, confused by his sudden change of attitude. 'This is what I'm doing here.' She lifted the book she held in her right hand and shook it at him when he looked over his shoulder.

He glanced at the book with something like contempt, then up at her face. 'So? You've seen the book. So what?'

'So what?' Her temper flared and blossomed before she had a chance to even think of controlling it, but even if she had she wouldn't have tried. After all, if anyone in this room had a right to be angry, she did. Whether or not she was grateful for what his photographs had shown her about herself, the fact remained that he had had no right to use them without permission. No right to use *her*, first for passing pleasure, and then for personal profit.

'So what?' she repeated, shouting now, and at least she had his attention. 'You had no right to use me this way!'

His body followed his head in the turn toward her, and a myriad of emotions altered his expression almost faster than Marnie could assimilate them—first astonishment, then disbelief, then anger. 'Use *you*?' he whispered.

She didn't have the slightest notion of what she would say next, but as it turned out a rehearsed speech would have been wasted. He had crossed the space between them before she could open her mouth to speak, then grabbed her arms and shook her once. 'Use *you*?' he repeated in a menacing growl, glaring down at her.

The unexpected, bruising physical contact had startled her, and all she could do was stare up at him, her eyes huge, her lips parted, uncertain of what would happen next or how she could prepare for it. She could feel his fingers pressing into the flesh of her arms, and an eternity seemed to linger in those few seconds before he snapped her against him and brought his mouth down on hers.

She was vaguely aware of the lingering scent of aftershave, the muted crackle of the arc lights cooling, but only vaguely. The angry, frustrated pressure of his mouth diminished all other sensations, pushing them far into the background of her awareness. She forgot the anger, the jealousy, the hurt; forgot even why she had come here. All she could think of was the way his chest flattened her breasts in a fierce, sweet ache; and how blissfully, willingly helpless she was against the strength of his hands. She felt the familiar, insidious warmth rise from the pit of her stomach and flood up through her breasts to her neck, and, unashamed, she lifted her arms away from his grasp and wrapped them around his neck.

He broke away with a startled gasp and knocked her arms down.

'You bitch!' he exhaled in astonishment, then his face went cold. 'You haven't changed a bit, have you? You can still turn it on and off at will.' His short bark of a laugh was bitter. 'It's an impressive talent, actually. I'd consider duplicating it, but I'm not sure I could live with myself.'

Marnie went perfectly still. She noted absently that her mouth was open, and forced it closed. 'What are you talking about?' she asked cautiously, as if she had cornered a wild animal, fearful that one wrong word would precipitate an explosion of violence.

'Hah!' He spun away and pretended snide applause, then began pacing back and forth in front of her, his eyes strangely alight. 'Very good, Marnie. A nice touch, that pretence of innocence, but then it was always very effective, wasn't it? Damned effective, up on the mountain. For a while there, you actually had me believing I'd penetrated that icy control of yours.'

He stopped in mid-stride, glaring at her, and his eyes seemed to smoulder beneath the dark shelf of lowered brows. 'It took me a long time to accept that I'd just been kidding myself. A hell of a long time. Marnie Weston doesn't need anybody, does she? She only pretends to, when it suits her.' His features softened suddenly, and so did his voice. 'I just can't get over how damn good at it you are.' Then he clamped his jaw shut impatiently, angry that he had permitted himself that one moment of vulnerability. When he spoke again, his tone was ice. 'How do you manage it, Marnie? How do people like you do it? Pretend such passion when you're feeling nothing?'

'Feeling nothing?' she repeated in a voice so small that he turned to look at her, his eyes narrowed in suspicion.

His lips were white from pressing them together, and she watched, fascinated, as colour flooded back into them. 'You left,' he said flatly, as if that answered everything. 'You couldn't wait to get away. I was back down in less than an hour, but even that wasn't fast enough.'

'Less than an hour?' She was starting to sound like a parrot, repeating everything he said, but she couldn't help herself. He couldn't have been back down in less than an hour. In order to do that he would have had to ride the gondola yet another time through the danger of the blizzard's winds, and why would he have done anything that stupid, when all he had to do was wait until late afternoon . . . ?

'Ross . . .' she took a step toward him, but his eyes warned her off.

'Stupid, wasn't it? But it seems I'm a master of stupidity. I had to advertise how stupid I was to the world,' he kicked viciously at the book, sending it sliding across the tile floor, 'just in case someone in some obscure part of the country hadn't heard. Even *Tiffany* felt sorry for me after she saw that. Can you believe it? Pity, from somebody like Tiffany!'

Marnie took a shaky breath and swallowed, totally

ignorant of how this incredible miracle had come to pass, but suddenly, stunningly aware that something had changed. That this silly man really *did* love her, and had somehow got the idea that she had rejected *him*.

'It's a beautiful book,' she said simply, not knowing what else to say, reaching out to touch his shoulder.

He jerked away furiously, and then, as if he had suddenly thought of something that hadn't occurred to him before, he turned toward her slowly, his eyes narrowed to slits, his mouth lifting in an unpleasant smile. 'What the hell am I doing?' he asked no one in particular. 'If this is all you want, by God, far be it from me to keep you from it.'

He was the personification of cold, calculating power as he moved toward her, his head lowered, black hair tumbling across his forehead. It surprised him a little that she didn't back away. She just stood there calmly, waiting, her eyes curiously bright, and that was what stopped him.

Suddenly Marnie found her voice and her thoughts, and the reason she had come—perhaps the reason for the rest of her life. 'Explain the dedication in that book,' she demanded breathlessly.

His eyes locked on hers with the bleak surprise of a man who has sustained an unexpected physical blow. 'Explain it?' he asked weakly. 'My God, what is there to explain?'

She licked her lips and breathed in as her mind and heart took that terrifying leap from the precipice of security. It was horrifying, and it was exhilarating: soaring into that emptiness of thought where one sacrificed control in exchange for the promise of things that might be. It wasn't so bad, really. What was the worst thing that could happen? He could say no, or, worse yet, he might laugh at her, but she could live through that, couldn't she?

'You love me,' she stated flatly. It wasn't phrased as a question, but it demanded an answer just the same.

'Past tense,' he retorted quickly, and her heart lifted higher and higher, riding the invisible currents of exaltation. He did. My God, he loved her.

Her smile was hard and fiercely bright, but her voice was soft, muting the accusation. 'You never said that. To Tiffany, to Bett, to all the women that just left this room, but you never said those words to me.'

'Of course I didn't!' he shouted. 'You made sure of that, didn't you?' He dropped his head for a moment, pressing the fingers of one hand to his temple, then jerked it up again, newly furious. 'You were the one woman I *couldn't* say that to, remember?' He shook his head and chuckled bitterly. 'The first time in my life those words would have had some meaning, and I couldn't say them aloud. Ironic, isn't it? I thought I'd explode with the need to say them, and then there you were, hovering over me when I woke up,' he closed his eyes and frowned, as if the memory were painful, 'so obviously worried that I *would* say them, demanding reassurance that I wouldn't . . .'

'What are you talking about?' she whispered.

His eyes chilled her. 'No strings attached, no conditions. Remember saying that? The first words out of your mouth.' He shook his head bitterly. 'They were my words originally, but you twisted their meaning and threw them back in my face. When I said them I meant that love isn't conditional, it's supposed to be a gift, not a burden. But that wasn't how you meant them, was it? You just wanted to remind me that you were back in control, and wanted no nasty, lingering involvement to mess up your perfect life.'

He glared at her furiously, his hands clenched at his sides, his eyes burning into hers.

Marnie's lips parted to speak, but the simple act of speech eluded her for a moment. 'No,' she said finally, shaking her head. 'That wasn't what I meant at all. I was just . . . repeating what you'd said . . . hoping . . . praying . . . that what had happened might have made a difference . . .' She took a deep breath and swallowed. 'It was a question, Ross,' she whispered, 'and you answered it, simply by repeating the words, as if they were some sort of a pact between us.'

His expression froze. 'What?' he whispered.

She closed the distance between them and lifted her hand to touch his cheek, prolonging the anticipation for as long as she could before she let her fingers graze the black shadow of his jaw.

He closed his eyes as if her touch were painful. 'But you left,' he reminded her, clinging to his bitterness, fighting the need to pull her into his arms.

'I had to.' Her hand was in his hair now, threading through the soft, glorious thickness of it, sending an electric current of pleasure back through her arm. 'You just wanted one more night, and I wanted so much more, more than I thought you could give.'

He tipped his head back and groaned. 'I wanted one more night to try to convince you that one more night would never have been enough, Marnie. But you never gave me the chance. All I could do was try to say it in the book.'

She looked up at him with dark eyes wide and brimming. 'You could say it now, you know.'

He lifted his chin away from her hand and closed his eyes. His nostrils flared slightly, and she saw the pulse pumping between the taut cords of his neck. 'I don't know the words for what I feel for you, Marnie,' he murmured hoarsely, reaching out blindly for the back of her neck, winding his fingers into the gloss of her hair, pulling her head gently backward.

She felt the quivering restraint in his hand, the violent tremble of the two fingers he used to tip her chin, and yet, for all the restrained strength she sensed, his lips were barely a whisper against hers. They fluttered against her mouth with surprising delicacy, snatching at the fullness of her lower lip, then pulling away, only to return and repeat the process again and again until her breathing broke in an irregular rush against his face.

'Dear God,' he gasped when she finally thrust herself against him, her arms twined around his neck as she breathed his name, over and over again, 'you need words, after *this?*'

She nodded silently, her hair brushing against his lips as he buried his face in the sweet fragrance.

He cradled her face in both hands and tipped it upward so she could see all he was saying with his eyes. 'All the words are old, Marnie,' he whispered sadly. 'I've said them all before . . .' Suddenly his face cleared and he smiled at her. 'I've just remembered a few I haven't used; a few words I've been holding in reserve . . . will you marry me, Marnie?'

She tipped her head back in the circle of his arm and felt the very last vestiges of control slip away as she smiled up at him, but before she could answer he rattled on quickly, almost apologetically, watching her face with worry, 'But you won't be marrying Ross Arnett, Fashion Photographer, I'm afraid. I'm leaving all that. Starting tomorrow, I'll be travelling the country from coast to coast, taking hundreds of pictures of farmers and mill workers and mothers and children . . .' He paused and sighed and his eyes seemed to warm and blur as they looked down on her. 'Real people. Important people. Like in my first book. People who fall in love and get married and have children, and make their mark in this world without ever having their faces on a magazine cover. That's all I've ever wanted to do, really, is take pictures of them. Will you marry a man with such a dream, Marnie?'

'I guess I'll have to,' she sighed happily, moving against him, then she lifted her head to smile up at him, and touched his lips lightly with one finger. 'Incidentally,' she said, 'I love you, and it might interest you to know that I haven't overused those words in my lifetime. I've been saving them for you.'

He stared down at her, his eyes full of the need to express in some shining, original phrase the feelings that were in his heart, but the only words he could think of were the old ones, the ones that lovers had been whispering to each other for centuries. 'I love you too, Marnie,' he murmured, a little surprised, because when he'd said them to her, they had sounded brand new.

'That goes without saying,' Marnie whispered, lifting her face for his kiss.

Coming Next Month

#1255 EVER SINCE EDEN Catherine George
Clemency falls in love with Nicholas Wood at a fancy-dress ball—a fact
confirmed the next day. There seems no reason their fairy-tale romance
shouldn't continue indefinitely So Clemency is devastated when, suddenly and
brutally, Nick changes his mind.

#1256 LAW OF LOVE Sally Heywood
Kim is bowled over by barrister Con Arlington's looks and charm—until she
discovers he is really Conan Arlington-Forbes, the man she's held a grudge
against for five years   with good reason!

#1257 ONCE A HERO Anne McAllister
Lesley had built a satisfying new life for herself before her husband, Matt
Colter, reappeared, causing her more pain than joy Matt had always put his
work before their marriage, and she has no reason to believe he's changed.

#1258 ELUSIVE AS THE UNICORN Carole Mortimer
Eve refuses to believe Adam when he says she'd be making a mistake marrying
Paul. Even though their names seem to indicate an affinity between them,
Adam is a total stranger and has no right to interfere in her life.

#1259 BLACK LION OF SKIAPELOS Annabel Murray
When Helena meets Marcos Mavroleon she isn't looking for a relationship,
simply trying to mend a broken heart. His complex personality draws her
close—yet his traditional streak means that he can never be hers.

#1260 TASMANIAN DEVIL Valerie Parv
Evelyn agrees to fend for herself for a month on a tiny island—to prove herself
capable to her father Expecting to be alone, she finds the enigmatic Dane
Balkan already there. He seems as unhappy with her presence as she is with his.

#1261 SKIN DEEP Kay Thorpe
Tessa enjoys working with children but makes it a rule never to get emotionally
involved with her charges. In her present case, though, it isn't young Jason
causing her upsets, but his attractive, aggressive father, Mark Leyland.

#1262 GUARDIAN ANGEL Patricia Wilson
Tara dislikes her overpowering boss, Ben Shapiro, even though she's grateful
for his kindness to her disabled mother It does seem strange, though, that
every time she meets Ben, sparks fly between them.

Available in April wherever paperback books are sold, or through
Harlequin Reader Service:

In the U.S.
901 Fuhrmann Blvd.
P O Box 1397
Buffalo, N.Y 14240-1397

In Canada
P O Box 603
Fort Erie, Ontario
L2A 5X3

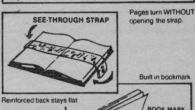

Harlequin *Superromance*®

LET THE GOOD TIMES ROLL . . .

Add some Cajun spice to liven up your New Year's celebrations and join Superromance for a romantic tour of the rich Acadian marshlands and the legendary Louisiana bayous.

CAJUN MELODIES, starting in January 1990, is a three-book tribute to the fun-loving people who've enriched America by introducing us to crawfish étouffé and gumbo, zydeco music and the Saturday night party, the *fais-dodo*. And learn about loving, Cajun-style, as you meet the tall, dark, handsome men who win their ladies' hearts with a beautiful, haunting melody. . . .

Book One: *Julianne's Song*, January 1990
Book Two: *Catherine's Song*, February 1990
Book Three: *Jessica's Song*, March 1990

Harlequin Presents...

CAROLE MORTIMER

Award of Excellence

elusive as the unicorn

*When Eve Eden discovered that Adam
Gardener, successful art entrepreneur, was
searching for the legendary English artist, The
Unicorn, she nervously shied away. The Unicorn's
true identity hit too close to home....*

*Besides, Eve was rattled by Adam's
mesmerizing presence, especially in the light
of the ridiculous coincidence of their names—
and his determination to take advantage of it!
But Eve was already engaged to marry her
longtime friend, Paul.*

*Yet Eve found herself troubled by the different
choices Adam and Paul presented. If only the
answer to her dilemma didn't keep eluding her....*